Heavenly Realm Publishing
Houston, Texas

ISBN—978-1-9839969-5-8

Library of Congress Control Number—2012932789

This book is printed on acid free paper.

Printed in the United States of America

Published By: **Heavenly Realm Publishing**
16760 Hedgecroft Dr., Suite 614
Houston, Texas 77060
Toll free: 1-877-599-3237
Fax: 281-520-4059

She's Mine

a novel

LaJohna Newbould

Dedications

First of all, I would like to dedicate this book to God (Father, Son, and Holy Spirit), without whom it never would have been written. What a journey I have had with Him as we have traveled through each page. I have so enjoyed every surprising moment of it.

Second, I would like to thank my husband, Jimmy, for all of his hard work, sometimes working all day and late into the night, to see this book come to fruition.

To The Reader

As with any endeavor we decide to undertake, we begin with baby steps; learning as we go. Step by step through trial and error; never giving up. Each trial makes us stronger. Each error, once found, gives us an opportunity to correct it.

My learning session is over for the time being. I hope you enjoy my stumbling attempts to take the path I believe God placed before me.

May God Bless You

Table of Contents

Chapter One

He watched her swim just as he had done every morning for the last two weeks. Even though he didn't know why someone had hired him to kill her, he was beginning to enjoy this daily routine. But now, he needed to come up with a plan. He needed to find out the one thing that she did the same time every day, but so far that had not happened. She didn't seem to have a timetable; a routine? Yes! A timetable? No! She may do the same things day after day, but she never repeated what she did in the same order. So for now he would just watch; watch and wait.

Chloe had gotten into the habit of swimming every morning since she and her husband, Seth, bought an above-ground swimming pool several weeks ago; which at the moment was all they could afford. It was four-feet high and twenty-four feet in diameter. Maybe sometime in the future they would be able to get an in-ground pool, but for now this pool worked just fine.

She climbed up the ladder on the one side and then she turned around and stepped down the ladder on the other side, easing herself into the water. It was cool and she loved the coolness as her body, then her head slowly went under the water. When she surfaced, she started to swim.

ॐ

The woods gave him the cover he needed so he could watch her for as long as he pleased. He had watched her long enough to know she was beginning to start her morning routine.

1

She would get in the pool and swim slowly from side to side. Sometimes she would swim across once, twice, but he never really knew how many times. She would stop at the ladder then she would walk so many times in one direction, stop, turn, then walk so many times in the other direction. At some point she would stop by the ladder and start to swim from side to side again. She would swim away from the ladder then when she reached the other side, she would stand up, raise her hands high above her head as if she was reaching for the sky, then lie down backwards in the water and start her backward swim toward the ladder. When she reached the ladder, she would stand up and swim forward to the other side. She would repeat this time, and time, again until she got tired.

He didn't have all the kinks worked out yet, but he had finally come up with a plan. The plan was to wait until she had been in the pool for a while. He wanted to catch her as she came up for air when she reached the side of the pool away from the ladder. She would not be expecting him to be there and would barely have time to gasp for air before he grabbed her and pushed her head back under the water. She would be tired and would not be able to fight back, and if she did, it would not be for very long. But so far he had not managed to be in the right place at the right time.

She stopped swimming and looked in his direction several times. He knew that he was hidden by the brush, so he just stood and watched her. After staring in his direction for several seconds, she turned and continued to swim.

He didn't know why someone wanted her dead, but it didn't really matter. He needed the money. So he watched and waited for the moment he would act. Whoever it was wanted it done, and done now. Even though this wasn't the way he usually worked, he was being paid. So at this time he would do it the way he was being paid to. He took pride in his work and if he got some pleasure along the way; that was okay too.

2

Chapter Two

C hloe was finished with her swim for the day, but as she got out of the pool, she stopped and tried to look deep in the woods to see if anyone was there. She stood for several moments listening because she had this feeling deep in her bones that someone was watching her. "Why would anyone be way out here?" she thought. She didn't know, but she also didn't know why anyone would be watching her.

She stepped off the ladder, grabbed her towel, and went into the house. Just before she closed the sliding glass door that led from the patio into the kitchen she took one last look into the darkness of the woods. She felt cold and as her body shivered, she pulled the door shut. Usually she shut the door without a moment's hesitation as to whether it was locked or not, but this time she made sure she locked it. She stood looking out the door and then reached out and pulled the curtains shut. She was afraid. She didn't like the feeling, but it was there nonetheless.

CB

He saw her movement and laughed to himself. In the two weeks he had been watching her, this was the first time she locked the door. Though he was amused at her actions, he also knew the time had come for him to act. The more she became aware of his presence, the more she would start to take precautions. Then he would have lost his edge.

Chloe got up early the following morning to go swimming. The coolness of the water felt good as she started her morning routine. After she swam for a while, she began to feel uncomfortable. She felt a presence today more than any other day. Last night she tried to tell her husband about how she was feeling, but he didn't take her seriously. In a way, she couldn't blame him. It did sound pretty far-fetched. Nevertheless, the feeling was still there and she could not get rid of it. No matter how hard she tried, she could not think of a reason why someone would be in the woods behind their house watching her.

Chloe and Seth had bought five acres of land about twenty miles from town. Their house was located at the back of their property. Most of the land was in front, but there was one-half acre on each side which made their place somewhat isolated. The back of the house was right up against the woods. Chloe loved living in the country and even though they had neighbors, they weren't on their front doorstep. In fact, they had made friends with many of the families that lived in the area.

They had even started going to a small country church that was located about five miles down the road. Several of the families they met went there and she enjoyed being part of the congregation.

The woods behind the house belonged to a forest preserve. Someone bought the rights to the deer lease in that area, plus there was an oil rig, but other than that there was no reason for anyone else to be there. She didn't go back there, and she knew very few people that even wanted to go in those woods.

She and Seth lived in town before they decided to buy some land and move out of town. Now she loved the quietness this afforded them. She liked the peace she felt as she sat outside and listened to the birds singing. However, her neighbors had cows and she could hear them in the distance, especially when it was feeding time. Once the cows saw the truck and knew they were going to be fed they made lots of noise; very loud noise! But, in a way all the sounds of the animals were comforting.

Lately there was an uneasiness that she could not explain. The peace she once reveled in now eluded her. So she got out of the pool and went back into the house. She got herself a cup of coffee and sat down at the kitchen table. Not able to really focus on any one thing she just sat there and let her mind wander trying to figure out when she first started feeling this unease.

ભ

With a pair of binoculars the man was able to see her face as if he was sitting across the table from her. As he watched, he could see the different emotions as they played across her face. He could also see the fear as her eyes slowly went back and forth scanning the trees. He knew she was trying to figure out why someone would be watching her and if there was a reason behind the way she felt, or if it was just her imagination.

She got up and got herself another cup of coffee, then went and stood gazing out at the woods. Then she reached out and closed the curtains before she returned to the table, sitting there in complete silence. She was on high alert. She didn't know why, but she was. She wanted to swim, but the fear she felt kept her from going outside and doing just that.

Chapter Three

Chloe did not swim for a couple of days because of the fear that was beginning to consume her. Nonetheless, this morning she decided it was time for her to get past that fear and go for a swim. She wasn't even sure she had a reason to be afraid.

The above ground pool she swam in was just what he needed, because as she swam, she could not see what was going on just outside of the pool on the ground; but it was also a problem for him, because he couldn't see in the pool to be sure where she was at any given time.

He had been watching her for over two weeks now and each day he had edged a little bit closer. This morning he was just a few feet beyond the beginning of the woods. He could feel his body reacting to her nearness. He was closer than he had ever been before and he liked it.

She stopped swimming and looked his way. He knew she couldn't see him, but he stood very still just in case. She stood for several moments looking in his direction, but then she turned and continued swimming. He breathed a sigh of relief.

Chloe finished her swim and now sat in the chair in the living room. Even though the T.V. was on, she didn't watch it. She didn't know whether to tell her husband or not. She was afraid he would dismiss her fear just as he had done once before. She knew how she felt, but could not explain it to him so he would understand.

As she sat there feeling so lost and alone, her thoughts went to God. She reached for her Bible, which she kept on the table beside her chair, but before she could even open it, a bible verse came to her mind. It was found in Hebrews 13:5. *"I will never leave thee, nor forsake thee."*

She meditated on that verse for several minutes, and as she did, a peace settled over her so that she thought she would be able to get up and go about her day. She had quite a few things she needed to accomplish and sitting here worrying about a problem, she may or may not have, was not helping anything at all.

But instead of getting up, Chloe went down on her knees to pray,

"Lord, I know you know all things and I know you know whether the reason behind this fear is real or not. I put my life in your hands. Help me Lord. Amen."

C3

He smiled at the fact she had gone to her knees in prayer. At first, he wasn't quite sure what she was doing, but on seeing her hands placed together in front of her face, he knew. If she thought a little prayer was going to help her, she was going to be very surprised at how wrong she was.

Chapter Four

It was the beginning of another day and he was already in place. After yesterday and the way she had reacted, he wasn't sure she would go swimming today; but here she was. She probably thought the prayer she said yesterday was going to help. How wrong she was.

ᨠ

Chloe started her ritual swim. She had always felt invigorated as she swam, but today was different. Once again, she felt uneasy and fearful. She didn't understand what was going on.

"Oh, Lord. What is wrong? I'm afraid. I look into the woods and I don't see anything, but I still feel as if someone is watching me. Why? I don't understand."

Chloe stopped her swim and stared off into the woods. The uneasiness she felt was so intense. More so than at any other time. So intense it was actually making her sick to her stomach. Even though she wasn't through she decided to stop early. She went into the house and again locked the door behind her.

ᨠ

He was angry, very angry. Today he made it so close to the side of the pool he could actually touch it. He crouched there waiting for her to come up for air, and he placed himself in the area straight across from the ladder knowing he could not be seen from the house. He didn't know if her husband was home or not, but today was the day. Today he was at least going to try.

She had swam long enough for him to know she was getting tired. She was also breathing hard, which made it perfect for her to not put up much of a fight.

Then out of the blue she stopped. She went straight to the ladder and got out. She went into the house and locked the doors. Now, why did she do that?

CX

Chloe sat alone in her living room. Her husband had already gone to work. Why didn't he believe her? She didn't understand. There were so many things she didn't understand. She was afraid, but of what? Her husband's attitude confused her. Why?

After a while she got up and started going about her daily routine. She knew what needed to be done and she did everything, but she did it out of habit.

She cried a little because she was so upset her husband refused to give credence to her intuitiveness. She knew how strange it sounded, but so far he hadn't even given her the benefit of the doubt, and that hurt. When she explained how she felt, she thought he might at least go take a look; but he didn't.

She wondered if the police would take her seriously, but if her own husband wouldn't, why would anyone else?

Chapter Five

"Darla, would you like to go shopping today? I am so tired of being up here without anything to do. I guess I'm just getting cabin fever. How about it?"

"Chloe, it sounds good to me. Shopping is my forte. Why don't we go to the mall in Humble and just make a day of it? We can eat at the food court and of course we can shop as long as we want before we get tired."

"Great! I'll pick you up in a few minutes." Chloe put the phone down wondering if she should say anything to Darla about what she was feeling. She decided not to because she didn't want to scare her.

But then, just before she pulled into Darla's drive, she decided she might mention it but would wait to see if the opportunity presented itself. She didn't want to cause Darla any concern, but she also did not want Darla to be oblivious to a threat right here in their neighborhood; if there was one. She really did not know one way or the other.

So as they drove to the mall, Chloe talked to Darla trying to feel her out as to whether she had seen anything strange in the neighborhood lately. The only thing Darla could think of was the dogs barking late one night. She had gotten up and looked around, but the dogs quieted down so she went back to sleep.

He stood trying to decide what to do. She had left and he didn't know how long she would be gone. That woman could be so frustrating. She never kept on any time schedule. She came and went and he never knew when, or where, or for how long. Her movements were completely unpredictable, which is what made killing her so hard. He had been in position the other day and all of a sudden she just stopped and got out of the pool.

It had now been over three weeks and he could not find anything either one of them did on a regular schedule. He had gotten so involved in watching her he had slipped up and not found out who her husband worked for. Now he would have to take time to do something he should have done in the first place.

Chapter Six

D arla and Chloe went from shop to shop. Chloe had finally relaxed and was having a good time. She looked at Darla and told her "I am exhausted. Let's go to the food court and get something to eat. We can also put our feet up and rest."

"Sounds like a great idea to me." Darla said as she placed her packages on top of an empty table.

"I am absolutely starving. If you will watch the packages, I will go and get us something to eat. What do you prefer?"

"If you'll go and get it, I'll eat whatever you decide to get. I'm hungry but I think I'm more tired, so being tired wins out. I'll sit. You go find us something to eat. Please!"

Chloe could see Darla standing in line at the Mexican restaurant so she sat back and put her feet up on the chair in front of her. As she sat there relaxing and waiting for Darla to bring the food, she started getting the feeling that she was being watched. "It can't be, please God." She made herself calm down, but at the same time, she started looking around to see if anyone was watching her. She didn't move her head. Slowly she moved her eyes back and forth trying to locate the cause of her uneasiness, but she didn't see anything. She leaned back in her chair trying to give the impression she was relaxed, but her eyes were continually on the move. Again she didn't see anything. One more turn and she came face to face with Darla.

"What are you doing? You look so intent; you would think someone was after you or something."

Chloe jumped when she came face to face with Darla. "Darla, you just scared the life out of me!"

Chloe had so far not told anyone what was happening in her life. Her husband didn't believe her so why should anyone else. Darla sat the food on the table. "Sorry, Chloe, I didn't mean to scare you. I was watching you as I stood in line and you seemed so intent on what you were doing that I thought it might be fun….Oh, Chloe, I am so sorry because from the look on your face it was anything but fun. I am so sorry!"

After they finished eating, both Chloe and Darla decided it was time to go home. They had had enough for one day. The day was over and they were tired so they didn't talk much on the way home.

Chloe dropped Darla off at her house and headed home, but as she started up the drive, she thought she saw a shadow off to the side of the house where the swimming pool was. When she stopped in front of the garage doors, she just sat there; not wanting to get out of the relative safety of the car. How long she sat there, she didn't know. When her husband pulled up beside her, he walked over to her window and knocked on it. She turned and looked at him with such fear in her eyes that at first he was taken aback. She looked at him and just burst into tears. As he looked at her, he immediately remembered all the times she had tried to tell him she was afraid and that she felt someone was watching her. Now that he looked into her tear streaked face he was filled with remorse. He should not have dismissed his wife's concerns so easily.

It was almost dark when Chloe and her husband walked into the house from the garage. They had each pulled their cars into the garage, got out and went into the house pushing the button that closed the garage doors behind them. They then locked the door between the house and the garage. Seth and Chloe went in and sat down on the double recliner in the living room. He held her as she tried to explain what had been happening over the last three weeks. Then she finished with what happened at the food court in the mall, and the shadow she thought she had seen when she was pulling up to the house. Chloe felt better now that Seth at least listened to her.

She slept soundly in her husband's arms and woke up early the next morning. She pulled her swimsuit on and headed out to the pool. She thought maybe, because it was so much earlier than usual that maybe, just maybe, whoever was watching her would not be out there this early. Chloe once again started her ritual swim; swimming back and forth several times, walking to the left several times, stopping and walking to the right several times. Now she would repeat each session until she was tired, hopefully for at least an hour, and then she would go into the house.

ᘓ

He watched her as she started her routine. As she swam, he slowly moved closer and closer to the side of the pool facing away from the house. There he crouched down waiting for her.

There were times when her hands reached the side of the pool, the water from her hands would sprinkle over and get his head wet. It wasn't much, but just enough to let him know how close she was; but then she went into a backward swim and he wasn't fast enough to grab her. He practiced grabbing her hand when he thought the time was right, but so far his timing was off.

ᘓ

As Chloe swam, she prayed. This morning before coming out to swim she replayed the events from yesterday from the moment she felt eyes on her in the food court to the moment she saw the shadow from the drive. Back and forth, she swam, but now she was getting tired. One more time she decided and she would quit for today.

14

He crouched down waiting for her hand to appear. It would happen any second now. He waited. He knew she was getting tired and as soon as he saw her hand touch the side of the pool, he would put his hand on hers so she couldn't pull away. Then he would push her head under the water. He could hear her splashing the water as she came his way. He was poised and ready for action. This was the day.

"Chloe, Chloe, Chloooe., are you ready for breakfast?" Her husband yelled as he stepped out onto the patio walking toward the pool. After last night, he decided to take a day off and now he stood waiting for her to return to the side of the pool with the ladder. As she grabbed hold of the opposite side of the pool to make her turn, she once again splashed the man waiting out of sight crouched down near the pool.

Hearing her husband's voice, she stopped. Her head turned in his direction with a questioning look on her face.

The man stood completely still, stopping in mid action. She was standing right above him talking to her husband and he could do nothing. She was in the perfect position and he could do nothing. He was so close. He didn't move. He waited.

He could not believe his bad luck. Once again she had eluded him. He had been so close and then the opportunity had so quickly been taken out of his hands. Anger filled every pore of his being as he crouched there. He sat on the back of his heels waiting for them to go back into the house. She was his. He could wait.

"What?" Chloe said as she realized her husband was calling her.

"I just wanted to let you know breakfast was ready if you wanted some?"

Smiling Chloe said, "You betcha! What's on the menu?"

"Eggs, bacon, and toast. How does that sound?"

"Sounds good to me. Just give me a minute to get out of the

pool." Chloe said as she swam toward the ladder.

"Hold on just a minute and I'll help you. The ladder is a little wobbly." Taking her by the hand Seth helped her get down the ladder and then they walked toward the house.

"I sat our breakfast on the patio table. With the weather being so nice I thought you might like sitting outside."

∽

As they sat down outside, the man crouched behind the pool. He had almost made a mistake. He had assumed when her husband said he made breakfast that they would go in the house. So he stood up getting ready to run into the woods, but they didn't go in the house because her husband had put breakfast on the patio. If they had been facing a different direction, they would probably have seen him. Now he was stuck for the time being. He couldn't take the chance that either one of them would see him as he ran back into the woods.

The man listened as Seth and Chloe talked. He could hear them quite well, and smiled as Chloe once again told Seth about the feeling she had while she swam.

"Chloe, why don't you change into something else and we'll go check out the woods."

Chloe jumped up to go in the house and Seth's phone rang. He was on call for his job so he answered his phone right away. He listened for a minute then nodded his head in agreement, even though the person on the other end of the line could not see the movement of his head. "Yes, I'll be there as soon as I can."

Chloe nodded her head, put her arms around him, and gave him a kiss saying, "I guess it will wait until tomorrow. Drive safe and I'll see you when you get home."

∽

Seth got up and went into the house. He needed to get ready to drive into Houston. He liked his job, but at times like this he wished he

16

was able to check out the woods first. He saw the relief on Chloe's face when he told her to go get dressed, but then the call came from his job. As he talked, he saw the look of disappointment as she realized he was going to have to go to work.

As Chloe continued to sit on the patio, Seth came out to say goodbye, "I am so sorry, Chloe. I promise we will check out the woods and the area around the pool when I get home."

"Promise?"

"Yes, I promise."

Seth bent and gave her a kiss, turning around he went through the house and out the front door as he headed toward his car. She heard the car door slam and knew he was gone.

℃ℨ

Her swim was over for today, but now he had a problem. If they went traipsing around in the woods behind their house, they would eventually find out where he was staying. As soon as she went inside, he would need to police his area, so to speak, so there wouldn't be anything to give his presence away.

Chloe had been praying for several minutes when she finally stood up and went into the house. She had decided once again that her life was in God's hands and she was not going to let her fear dictate her actions.

℃ℨ

As soon as the man heard the patio door close, he stood up and ran into the woods. He had a lot of ground to cover before her husband got home from work. It took him quite a while to pick up all the stuff he had dropped. He had to work slowly. He didn't want her to accidentally see him from the house, but he also had to make sure he wasn't seen from any other direction. Though their neighbors did not live close you never knew when one might be outside. He had policed the area as good as he could. Now he needed to locate her.

17

Evening was approaching and her husband should be coming home pretty soon. When that happened, he would need to leave. He couldn't take the chance they would spot him while they were checking out the area. Silently he sat just watching the house and waiting for something to happen.

He heard the phone ring, saw the woman as she walked across the room, watched her face as she listened to the person on the other end, and saw her disappointment when the other person stopped talking. Finally she said, "Seth, you said we could go check out the woods this evening. I know your job comes first, but I was really looking forward to at least seeing if there was anything there or not." She waited for a bit and finally said, "Well, I guess if you put it that way. When do you think you will be home? I guess I'll see you in the morning."

He was glad she left the window open. Otherwise, he would not know what was going on. He didn't know what time her husband was going to be home, but if her voice was anything to go by, it wasn't going to be very soon.

If she would just go swimming in the morning, he would have another try at bringing her life to an end. He needed the money he had been offered, but he didn't get it until she was dead. Once again, he wondered why someone wanted her dead, but again it didn't really matter. He was broke. He really needed the money, but things were not happening as fast as he thought they were going to in the beginning.

Chapter Seven

W here is she?" He thought as he wondered where she had been the last two days. He hadn't even seen her through the windows. The curtains had stayed the same. If the curtains were opened, they remained opened. If they were shut, they remained shut.

He had watched the house all day every day and nothing. He was back early this morning, but she had not yet come out to swim. If things were on schedule, she should be coming out any minute now. So he would wait and see.

ങ

An hour passed. Slowly the minutes continued to tick by. "Where is she?" He thought once again.

"Was that a movement by the patio door? Yes. Yes. It was. Wherever she had been she was back and now he could get on with his job.

He watched as she opened the door. She walked toward the pool, draped her towel over the ladder, and proceeded to climb up and then down on the other side. She ducked completely under the water and when she came up she started swimming. She swam for a while and then started her usual routine.

When Chloe had opened the patio door, she once again felt like she was being watched. She couldn't believe it. She and her husband had gone away for the weekend hoping that being gone for a short time would take away that awful feeling, but it didn't. Not even a little bit. Her first step on the patio had told her that. It was like she had never been away and she knew she was not alone.

CB

As she swam, he came out of the woods and once again hid himself close to the side of the pool facing away from the house waiting for the right moment. He listened as she swam. He could tell when she was swimming or walking. He also knew that ninety-nine percent of the time she would finish her routine; but now her routine was different.

She had been swimming for about forty-five minutes so he knew she was beginning to get tired. He placed himself straight across from the ladder; knowing this was generally the direction she swam.

Chloe's hand touched the side of the pool and the water dropped on his face. He stood up just as she pulled herself up gasping for breath. He reached out before she had a chance to surface and grabbed her hair pushing her face back under the water. She pushed away from the hand that held her captive. She tried to stand. She needed air and she needed it bad. She kept trying to pull free, but the person that held her under the water had his hands entangled in her hair, and she couldn't get away. Darkness threatened, but still she tried; and then nothing.

Chapter Eight

C hloe, where are you? Sorry I overslept." Seth called as he stepped out of the patio door. On hearing Seth's voice the man let go of Chloe's hand and hair and slipped into the woods behind the house before Seth came into view.

"Chloe, do you want to go to town and eat some breakfast?" As Seth got closer to the pool, he saw Chloe floating in the water face down.

"Oh, no! no! no!" He ran to the ladder and jumped into the pool. He rushed to Chloe's side grabbing hold of her arms. He layed her over the side where she was half in and half out of the pool. Bent at the waist, she was face down. Seth flipped himself over the edge then pulled Chloe's lifeless body over the edge so they both fell backwards on to the ground. He blew into her mouth then started CPR.

There was no one else around to help him so he continued alone. Just before he gave up, Chloe coughed, spit out a lot of water, and started breathing. Seth picked her up and ran to the car, and headed to the hospital as fast as he could.

ॐ

When they arrived at the hospital, he pulled up to the emergency room doors and honked his horn several times. He ran to Chloe's side of the car and started to pull her out just as a nurse came running out with a wheel chair. Seth explained what happened and at the same time put Chloe in the chair. The nurse pushed the wheelchair through the emergency room doors while calling for a doctor at the same time.

☙

He stood and watched as Seth picked up the woman and ran toward the car. He had failed again.

☙

After Chloe was checked out by the doctor, they decided to keep her overnight to make sure there were no after effects from her almost drowning. Her husband did not know how long she had been under the water and neither did she.

While she slept, Seth sat in a chair beside her bed. He was so very thankful that she was okay. At the same time he was angry because he had told her not to swim by herself. He watched her as she slept, and his heart was beating out of control. He had almost lost her.

He sat there for a long time watching her face. He tried not to think about what it would have been like if he had not gone outside when he did. He stared at her for the longest time, but finally fell asleep in the chair beside her bed.

☙

Early the next morning, Claire, the nurse on the morning shift, came in to let Seth and Chloe know that the doctor said she could go home. "Even though the doctor has said you can take her home, he also said to be sure to keep an eye on her for the next couple of days. As you know, she had a pretty close call."

"If you'll pull your car up to the front of the hospital, I'll push her down in the wheelchair and you can take her home."

On the way home Seth was very quiet. Finally he said, "Chloe, why do you insist on swimming by yourself. I asked you not to. Do you realize how close I came to losing you?"

"Seth, you have got to listen to me. Someone tried to kill me. You must have scared them away when you came outside to see if I wanted to go eat breakfast. I know it's hard to believe and I can hardly believe it's true myself. But it is. I swim by myself all the time. I'm careful; as careful as I can be, anyway. You've got to believe me. Someone tried to drown me. When I came up for air, after swimming across the pool, I started to pull myself up as I do when I'm getting ready to swim backwards to the other side and someone grabbed my hair and pushed me back under the water. I fought but I couldn't get his hands out of my hair so that I could get away. I told you I thought someone was watching me, but you wouldn't believe me. Do you believe me now?"

As they pulled up in front of the garage doors, Seth said "I don't know what to think anymore, Chloe. We're home. Let me help you into the house and get you comfortable and then I'll look around the pool and see if I can see anything. I'll come back and check on you, but I thought I might take a look in the woods while I'm at it. We didn't get a chance to do that the other day."

଎

Seth took Chloe in the house and made her comfortable on their double recliner. Then he went outside to do what he had told her he was going to do.

Chloe sat there trying not to cry. She had been so scared. She had come so close to dying and she wasn't even sure her husband believed her; but she knew. She no longer had any doubt. She remembered very clearly the feel of the man's fingers in her hair. She remembered how she had felt when she came up for air and there wasn't any. She remembered fighting, trying to get away from the person that held her under the water and failing. She remembered the blackness overcoming her and then nothing.

"Oh, God! Why is this happening to me? I don't understand what is going on. I am so afraid, and I don't even know if my husband believes me. I need your help."

As always, Chloe's Bible was lying on the table beside her. Just holding it made her feel better. So she started flipping through its pages hoping to find something to bring her comfort. Once again she came across the verse *"I will never leave thee, nor forsake thee."* She had highlighted this verse many years ago when she first read it. She liked it then and she liked it much more now. It was good to know that God was with her and that He wasn't going to leave her no matter what. She laid the open pages next to her heart as she closed her eyes.

Seth came back in the house through the patio door. He looked at his wife as she slept. He had come so close to losing her, and now it looked as if someone had tried to kill her. He picked up the phone and went into the other room so he could call the police. He didn't want to scare Chloe any more than she already was.

Chapter Nine

The police pulled up in front of Seth and Chloe's house. Seth went out to meet them so he could take them to the back of the house by the swimming pool. He knew they were going to have to ask his wife some questions, but he thought he would try and explain what she had told him. Then they could look around, and then talk to her.

ଓ

From his place in the woods, he saw the police arrive. He knew he had messed up, but he didn't really think her husband would call the police. "Now what?" he thought. "Everything was going all wrong, and he didn't think his employer was going to be too happy with him. At all!"

ଓ

"Chloe, wake up. Sweetheart, wake up."

"What do you want?" Chloe said as she slowly opened her eyes. Then she sat up straighter as she realized her husband was not alone.

"Chloe, I want you to meet Detective Bonner. I called the police once I looked around the pool and in the woods. I figured if they looked around, they would know whether we have a problem or not and it seems that we do."

"What do you mean?"

"Chloe, they looked around and found evidence someone has

been in the woods watching our house. I told them you had a feeling someone was watching you, but you didn't know for sure until he tried to drown you. They want to ask you some questions."

"What questions?" Chloe looked at Detective Bonner. "I'm really sorry, but I don't know how I can help you. For about three weeks or so, I have felt like someone was watching me. I would go out to swim and would just get this feeling. I wasn't sure in the beginning what it was. All I knew was that it made me very uncomfortable and I wanted to go back into the house. It was just a feeling."

Chloe looked at her husband wanting and needing his support, but she knew he had not believed her in the beginning and wasn't sure exactly where he stood right now. Seth looked at Chloe then went over and sat down beside her.

"Chloe, I am so sorry I did not listen to you before. I was so tied up with work I was only half listening to what you were saying. When I went outside and you were floating in the pool, I thought I had lost you. I have never been so scared in my life."

Chloe looked at Seth with tears in her eyes as Seth said,

"Detective Bonner, I think my wife needs to rest now. So if you don't mind, I'm sure she would like to curl up on the recliner and go to sleep. So I would like her to do just that. I will see you out."

Chloe pushed back in the recliner and closed her eyes. Seth lovingly put the blanket over her and then headed for the door with Detective Bonner.

"Detective, what do you think is going on? I almost lost my wife because I didn't believe what she was trying to tell me. That won't happen again."

"To tell you the truth I am not for sure. What we found at the pool could show signs of a struggle, but the imprints in the sand where it took place could also have just been you getting her out of

26

the pool and giving her CPR. But then we have her account of what happened and the fact that she almost died." Detective Bonner continued. "We also found a cigarette butt and a candy wrapper in the woods. We will have to wait and see if we get any information back on them. I'll let you know as soon as we get any results, but you might try and get your wife to see if she can remember anything else. I know she might not right now, but she might think of something later. Anyway, give it a shot. Sometimes different things will trigger a different memory. We might get lucky. Take care, Mr. Kelley, and unfortunately I will probably be seeing you sooner than later."

"Thanks, Detective. I really appreciate your help."

The Detective left and Seth went back in the house and closed the front door behind him. Chloe was still asleep on the recliner in the living room and evil returned to the darkness of the woods.

⚃

He was watching as the police, under the direction of the detectives, found a cigarette butt and candy wrapper. He thought he had found everything he left, but evidently he had not. Once again his employer would not be happy; sloppy, very sloppy.

All was quiet in the house. He continued to watch but there was no activity. He guessed they were probably resting. The man who had hired him was not pleased at all with his mistake. The man had given him a cell phone so that they could keep in touch. He didn't like the idea, but it wasn't his call. He had thought about not calling him but he seemed to know everything anyway. Not that he needed to know, but his employer had finally revealed the name of the woman and her husband, Seth and Chloe. He actually did not like knowing the name of his victim; somehow knowing made it harder to kill them when the time came.

He got in a position where he could see into the living room through the patio doors. He could see Seth watching T.V., while he periodically looked over to see how his wife was doing. He could also see her. She was still asleep.

He was going to have to come up with a whole new plan. With her near miss he didn't know if she would go swimming anymore or not and even if she did, she was probably not going to be swimming alone. Now her husband was going to be a complication, because he now believed her. He was also going to be on the alert; all because (he) had failed. How could things go so completely wrong?

He hated waiting, but now he was going to have to wait and see what the Kelley's were going to do. He would continue to watch from the woods and as he watched he was going to have to try and come up with a new plan.

Chapter Ten

He had been watching the house for over a week ever since Chloe had gotten out of the hospital. He had not seen her one time. Periodically he would see her husband. He would work in the yard or clean the patio, but he did not go near the pool; nor did he go very far from the house.

ೞ

Today Seth had already swept the patio; watered Chloe's plants and had even mowed the yard. Thankfully he and Chloe had cleaned the pool and added all the necessary chemicals the day before her drowning episode so that was one chore he didn't have to do.

Now as he approached the pool, he came face to face with the worst day of his life. He remembered coming out the back door and onto the patio then, going around the edge of the house and heading toward the pool. He had wanted to take Chloe out to breakfast that morning, but as he looked at the pool, he couldn't see her at first. Then he looked and his heart seemed to stand still because she was floating face down in the water.

He barely remembered getting her out of the pool. The only reason he knew he had was because she was lying on the ground in front of him and his clothes were soaking wet. For a split second, he had been at a loss of what to do, but then he started CPR. He thought he had lost her, but after several minutes she finally coughed, spit up lots of water, and started to breathe. He was then also able to breathe. He had been so scared.

"What was going on? Who was trying to kill his wife? And why?" So many thoughts were running through Seth's head. He decided to put off cleaning the pool for another day. Right now it was just not something he was ready to do. Besides, he needed to get back to Chloe and make sure everything was okay.

Seth also needed to call Calvin, his boss, to give him an update on what was going on; which was nothing. He knew he was going to have to return to work at some time, but right now that was the farthest thing from his mind. Calvin had let him work from home this past week, but at some point they would have to discuss his options because he still needed his job.

"Oh, God! Help! I need to make a living, but I can't leave Chloe at home when I go to work. What if that person, whoever he is, tries to kill her again? I don't know what to do. As much as I want to be her hero, I can't keep her safe. It's not in my power to do so. Please show me what I need to do." Seth prayed as he walked toward the house.

He stopped at the side of the pool and stared at the water. It looked so clear and inviting he could understand why Chloe liked to swim so much. The water's small movements was hypnotizing. He continued to stare and tried to harness his thoughts, but he just couldn't seem to follow any one thought to its conclusion. While staring at the water a scripture came to his mind. Proverbs 3:5. He and Chloe had leaned on this scripture many times during their marriage when things seemed to be going wrong, and right now things were definitely going wrong. *Trust in the Lord with all thine heart and lean not to thine own understanding.* Sometimes that was hard. Like right now for instance.

Chloe came outside in search of Seth before he could think about the scripture for very long. When she found him, he had such an intense look on his face she wasn't sure she wanted to interrupt his thinking. As she approached, she called out to him, "Seth, are you okay?" He was so deep in thought, at first he didn't hear her.

"Seth, can you hear me? Are you okay?" This time he heard her and looked up into her worried face. He put a smile on his face and noticed that she had her swimsuit on.

"I see you have decided to go swimming." He said, admiring her courage.

"I wondered how long it would take you to get back into the water."

"I guess I decided that if you were out here it was okay for me to swim. You are going to stay out here for a while; aren't you?"

"If you're going to swim, I'm going to be right here. I'll just do some yard work or something until you finish."

☙

The man watched as Chloe got into the pool. He saw the enjoyment on her face and knew that sometime soon she would start swimming again by herself. He just had to be patient. If he could just get the man that hired him to get off his back, he could get back to work.

He enjoyed watching her and this was a danger because he was becoming too attached. He wasn't for sure he wanted to kill her anymore; at least not right away.

All of a sudden, the man turned around looking from the right to the left. He started looking deeper into the darkness of the woods that surrounded him. He wasn't sure, but he felt as if someone was watching him. He didn't like it. To him it didn't matter that he had been watching Chloe for weeks. He saw how it had bothered her; but this was different. This was him. He wasn't sure who would be watching him, except maybe the man that had hired him.

He became very still and waited. He didn't know what he waited for, but he waited. After a while, he decided maybe it was his imagination so he turned toward the woman once again and began to watch her.

⚃

Chloe decided it was time to get out of the pool. She started up the ladder then turned to ask her husband, "I'm going in the house. Do you want to come in, too?"

"No, I think I'll work out here for a little bit. That is unless you think you need me."

"No, I'm fine," Chloe answered. "Would you like something to eat?"

"Sure."

"What would you like?"

"Whatever you want to fix will be just fine."

"I think I would like a big breakfast, eggs, bacon, and toast with butter sounds really, really good. How about it?"

"You're right. It does sound good. I think I'll even add some hash browns. I'll yell when it's ready." Chloe said as she headed toward the house.

Chapter Eleven

When Chloe got to the kitchen, the front door bell rang. She went to answer it and found Detective Bonner standing there.

"Good morning, Mrs. Kelley. May I talk to you and your husband for a minute?"

"Seth is outside doing some yard work, but if you'll wait a minute, I'll go get him."

"Let me go find him and then I'll bring him in with me and we'll talk," Detective Bonner said.

Detective Bonner walked outside in search of Mr. Kelley. He walked toward the pool, and as he walked, he looked toward the woods wondering if John Bledsoe happened to be out there watching the house.

"Seth, are you out here?" The detective yelled as he headed toward the pool area.

Detective Bonner could tell Mrs. Kelley had been swimming this morning because she still had her swimsuit on. He was glad she was able to put what had happened behind her, but he was sure the information that he was going to tell them would probably put a stop to that.

"Good morning, Detective. What brings you out here today? Actually that was probably a pretty dumb question. I'm sure it has something to do with the investigation. You probably have some, if not all, of the results back from the lab. Right?"

"Yes, but I think I need to talk to you and your wife at the same time."

Detective Bonner and Seth walked toward the house. As they opened the patio door, they could smell the bacon cooking.

"Boy, that sure does smell good. Would you like some breakfast, Detective?" Seth asked.

"You're right it does smell good, but I think we need to talk first."

Detective Bonner and Seth went into the kitchen and pulled the chairs out from under the kitchen table. Chloe looked over at them and she could see the concern in their eyes.

"Mrs. Kelley. I think we need to sit down and talk for a minute. I need to update you and your husband on what has been taking place. Even though it's more information than what we had in the beginning I'm not sure it is going to bring any comfort to you."

Chloe turned the burner under the bacon on low as she went to the kitchen table and sat opposite of both men so she could look them in the eye. She looked at the detective, "Would you like some coffee before we get started?"

"No, Mrs. Kelley, I don't think so. I think we had better just sit down so I can tell you what is going on. We got the results from the lab and the DNA shows that a man by the name of John Bledsoe was definitely in the woods. His fingerprints were also a match to some that we have on file. He's in the system and has been there for a while, but it doesn't necessarily mean he's the one that tried to kill you. Although in all probability, he is our perpetrator.

"He is suspected of stalking several women, but so far we have not been able to prove anything against him. So, Mrs. Kelley, you really need to pay attention to your surroundings at all times. It would be better if you took a friend with you wherever you go. I know that it is probably really inconvenient, but for a while I think that is your safest course of action; at least for the time being."

Detective Bonner continued talking, knowing they did not like what they were hearing; but he knew it needed to be said.

"He failed to kill you in the swimming pool so I'm not sure he will try there again, but you never know. He will probably be looking for some other place. At the same time don't ever rule anything out. He's out there and for some reason we think he has honed in on you. He's dangerous. So please be careful and always, I repeat always, be aware of your surroundings. I want to emphasize that if you feel threatened, please don't hesitate to call. I'll put a note in your file so whoever ends up getting your call will act immediately. I'll also give you my cell phone number. I'm afraid, Mrs. Kelley, that is all we can do until something happens."

Chloe stood up slowly. The eyes she had felt watching her now had a name, John Bledsoe.

"Detective Bonner would you like to stay for breakfast?" she asked as she turned up the burner on the stove under the bacon. She tried to act calmly, but her insides were churning. Her mind screamed, "Oh, swift. Now what?"

"Thank you for asking. But I think I better get back to the station. Oh, Mrs. Kelley, I forgot. This is a picture of John Bledsoe. It's not a new one, but it's the only one we have."

Chloe looked at it, but she did not recognize him. She took the picture then asked the detective if she could keep it. She thought if she looked at it every time she left the house, she would commit it to memory and would be prepared if she saw him or if he approached her.

"Sure", he answered as he turned toward the front door. "Seth, thanks for seeing me out. I know you looked at the picture. Did you happen to recognize the man in the picture?"

"No I didn't. Do you know the whereabouts of this John Bledsoe?" Seth asked as he walked Detective Bonner to his car.

"No I don't. He's under our radar right now. We haven't seen him but we have heard he's in town."

Seth watched Detective Bonner drive off. "Oh, Lord. Instead of getting better, everything seems to be getting worse. What am I going to do?"

Seth walked back into the house after seeing the detective to his car. He saw Chloe sitting at the kitchen table. He walked toward her holding out his arms and she readily stepped into them finding the comfort she so desperately needed.

They stood that way for several minutes; each one drawing the strength they needed from the other one. They pulled apart and looked into each other's eyes. "Seth, what are we going to do?"

"We are going to pray. That's what we're going to do. We are so "not" in control of this situation."

Chloe and Seth grabbed each other's hands and bowed their heads. For a moment they just stood there in silence, neither one knowing what to say.

Finally, Seth broke the silence. "Lord God. Once again you are the one we come to when our trial is so big that we have no control over what is happening. This situation has taken its toll on both of us. I cannot stay off work indefinitely. Chloe cannot stay at home alone until this person is caught. In our hearts we know we are safe in your hands, but sometimes it's hard to let go and let you do your thing. Lord, we simply ask you to show us the way. Amen."

They both turned toward the recliner. They sat down and simply cuddled in each other's arms. Even though Chloe had fixed breakfast neither one of them felt much like eating.

CB

It never ceased to amaze him how many people left their curtains open. He watched as they prayed together and then as they went to sit on the couch.

He didn't believe in God and he never had. He had always wanted a relationship like the one they seemed to have, but for some reason that kind of relationship had always eluded him. Watching from a distance, he envied them.

This job was taking far too long. It seemed as if everything was going against him. Things kept getting in his way keeping him from finishing his assignment. Therefore, he wasn't going to get paid.

He knew the man that had hired him was getting impatient, but he didn't know what else to do.

Chapter Twelve

C harlie watched John while John watched Chloe. This was even better than stalking by himself. He received the same thrill as he did when he was the one doing the stalking, but this time he was able to relive it more than once. He watched as John day by day got closer to the pool until he finally reached the edge. He could see John as he crouched down within touching distance, but Chloe could not see John.

Charlie was thankful John did not have the same amount of intuitiveness as Chloe. He enjoyed watching him as he worked toward completing his task. He didn't know if fun was the actual word or not, but it was "fun" to watch John put a plan into action and then have it thwarted for some reason or another.

He felt John's frustration each time he got close, but there was also a thrill when he missed. He especially enjoyed watching when John finally raised himself up from the side of the pool as he made his move to kill Chloe. He lived those moments from afar as John put his hand on hers to keep her from pulling away. He almost received the same satisfaction when at the same time he put his other hand in her hair and shoved her head under the water. He watched as she fought, but she was so tired from swimming she did not fight for long. Then she quit fighting at all.

He felt the same frustration as John did when Seth came out and found his wife floating in the pool. He watched as Seth vaulted over the edge pushing and pulling her out of the pool and performing CPR on her until she spat out the water and started breathing on her own. He watched as Seth put Chloe in the car and sped away to the hospital.

Charlie had seen it all from beginning to end. He felt the same accomplishment and thrill at ending someone's life as he did when he had actually done the killing himself. The only difference was, now when the deed was done, he would suffer none of the consequences.

He left evidence for the police to find incriminating John. He watched as John very carefully picked up all his cigarette butts and candy wrappers, but after he left, Charlie went back and dropped one of each for the police to find. After John and Charlie met the last time, Charlie made sure he picked the things that would have John's fingerprints and DNA on them so he would be able to leave something in the woods.

Eventually they would arrest him and John would claim someone hired him, but they would find no evidence to support that theory. John would be arrested, and Charlie would go free.

Chapter Thirteen

Seth and Chloe were in the living room, and Seth was feeling very frustrated. Finally he said, "They haven't found John Bledsoe yet, so if he is still out in those woods, he knows now that his plan to kill you didn't succeed. Even though the police searched the whole area, doesn't mean he didn't return after they left. I know they're on the lookout for him, but what do we do in the meantime."

"We've prayed so now we need to take action and allow God to guide our steps." As Seth looked at Chloe, he asked, "Any ideas?"

Chloe had no ideas. At this point fear was uppermost in her mind. She knew she believed in a loving God. She also knew that she trusted Him; but right now all she could think about was this man, that she did not even know, was out there and he wanted her dead.

She laid back in her recliner. Her mind wandering here and there. Had she missed something over the last several weeks or so that would cause this man to be after her. Had she seen something she shouldn't have. Though her mind tried to relive her movements, she could not, once again come up with anything. Finally her mind just shut down as she fell asleep.

It was not a restful sleep. It was a sleep filled with John Bledsoe chasing her. Several times he almost caught her, but she would wake up just as he was getting close. She awakened so many times she finally decided just to get up.

Everything around her was quiet and still. Seth had fallen asleep in the recliner beside her and he didn't look as if he was sleeping any more peacefully than she had been. She meandered into the kitchen not knowing what else she wanted to do, so she made herself a cup of coffee. She wasn't worried about not sleeping. She didn't want to sleep.

Chloe didn't turn any lights on. She knew where everything was anyway. She took her cup into the living room wondering when night had fallen. Looking at her husband as he slept she decided not to wake him. Just because she couldn't sleep didn't mean she should wake him up just to keep her company. Although she was tempted.

She walked over to the patio door and stood looking out into the darkness beyond. She stood very still knowing she could not be seen because the house was as dark inside as it was outside. Both she and her husband had fallen asleep during the daylight hours so they had not turned any lights on.

As Chloe stared in the direction of the woods, she thought she caught sight of the glow off of a cigarette. It reminded her of a firefly, but this glow did not move. It stayed in one place. There were times it would get brighter and then it would look like it was almost going out. She was rooted to one spot as she stared out her patio door into the darkness. It was hard to believe the man, who was stalking her, this John Bledsoe, would have the temerity to stand so close to the house, but there he stood. At least she thought so, or was it her imagination? Did she really know for sure what she was looking at? If she believed he was out there watching the house, was she positive he could not see her standing in the doorway, and if he could see her, shouldn't she move?

"Why was he stalking her? Did a stalker even have to have a reason? Did he see her one day somewhere, and decide she was going to be the one?" All these thoughts were racing through her mind as she stood there staring into the woods.

Chloe continued to stand there mesmerized by the glow. Then all of a sudden, it wasn't there anymore. Had she or had she not seen it? She went and got herself another cup of coffee and returned to the door and just stared out the door in the direction where she thought she had seen the glow before. She almost decided it was her imagination when she saw a flicker of light brighter than the rest. Then the glow returned.

"Seth....Seth," softly she called her husband's name. She waited a few seconds. He didn't move so she called again. "Seth....Seth would you wake up! He's out there!"

Seth on hearing Chloe's voice sat up. "Chloe, where are you?"

"I'm right here by the patio door. Someone is out there at the edge of the woods. I can see the glow from his cigarette and I think I also saw him light it.

Seth got up and went to stand by his wife. Staring into the darkness in the direction she indicated he let his eyes adjust so he could see whatever she was seeing. He tried but he could not see what she saw.

"Seth, I'm going to call Detective Bonner. I don't care whether you see it or not. I can. I have been over here watching for the last several minutes. At first I wasn't sure either, but at one point I saw him finish with one cigarette then light up another one and now he's just standing there watching the house. Do you think he can see us?"

"Chloe, I don't know if he's out there, but if he is, this house is dark enough that, no, I don't think he can see us." Seth answered in a low voice.

"Then let's just stand here and watch. Try to focus in the direction I told you to look. Since you can't see the glow, maybe if we're lucky, he will have to light up another cigarette. I guess we need to wait and be sure before we call Detective Bonner. What do you think?" Chloe said.

As they stood there and waited, sure enough the cigarette glow went out.

"Seth, I think he just put it out, because I can't see the glow anymore. Just keep looking in that direction and maybe he will light another one." Chloe pointed in the direction she wanted Seth to look. They stood and they waited; and nothing.

"Just a little bit longer," Chloe whispered.
They were almost ready to give up when they both saw the flicker of light in the direction they were staring. "Seth, did you see it? Did you see the flicker of light? Please tell me you saw it."

"Actually, Chloe, I did see it and it looks like it could have been someone lighting a cigarette. That's enough. I'm not taking any more chances."

Seth backed out of the room and went to another room so he could be sure whoever it was in the woods would not be able to see the glow from his phone, or per chance be able to hear his voice.

Detective Bonner was close to the top of the call list on his phone. He pushed the send button, listened for the ring, then waited for him to pick up. He didn't, and it went to voice mail.

Frustrated, Seth closed the lid on his phone causing it to disconnect. Then he pulled up the number of the police department and again he pressed the send button and listened while it rang. Finally Detective Chin answered and Seth told him who he was and why he was calling.

At first Detective Chin gave him the run around, but after he pulled Chloe's case file up on the computer, he immediately called for two units to head to their location. He told Seth Kelley that he was on his way and for him to stay in the house and give the police a chance to do their job.

Seth went back to Chloe and they both stood there and waited for the police to arrive. They moved back into the kitchen as the morning light first started to show on the horizon.

They both stood glued to the patio door waiting for the police to arrive. They had been standing there for several minutes when they both saw the shadow move and knew their chances of the police getting there in time to catch him was just about nil.

Seth decided they had waited too long to call and he knew it was his fault. He hadn't believed Chloe in the beginning, and now it might be too late.

Again, the shadow moved and if they had not been standing there, they would never have seen it. Nor would they have even been sure someone was there. It was the shadow of a man.

Seth moved to the patio door. Chloe questioned him "What do you think you are doing? The police will be here soon let them take care of it."

"Chloe, I can't just stand here and do nothing. He hopefully doesn't know that we know he's out there so maybe I have a chance to surprise him."

"Yes, you may surprise him, but what if he has a gun?"

"Chloe, this is your life we're talking about. I can't just stand here and do nothing. Lock the door behind me."

Seth opened the patio door as quietly as he could and headed in the direction they had seen the shadow. As the sun continued to rise, the shadow was no longer there. It was definitely the form of a man and now he was on the run. He saw Seth open the patio door and he took off running away from the house. Now they were both running and crashing through the trees.

Seth was gaining on the man when he stumbled over a tree root that was sticking up out of the ground. He jumped up and continued to run in the direction he last saw the man, but now he was nowhere in sight.

He heard a car start up in the distance. It whizzed by him just as he reached the old dirt road that ran behind their house. The road was mainly used by the men who worked on the oil rig located in the woods behind their house. It was also used by those who were deer hunting, but that was only periodically. Seth watched as the tail lights disappeared in the distance.

He turned around and started walking back toward the house. Trudging through the woods he was extremely disappointed that he had lost the man. He figured the man was John Bledsoe, but he couldn't swear to it. He hadn't seen him well enough, but the man, whoever he was, had no business watching their house.

Seth walked toward the house, and as he walked, the hairs on the back of his neck stood up. For the first time in his life, he felt as if someone was watching him.

The thing was, he had been watched many times. His job required that he make instant decisions. He knew not everyone would agree with those decisions but because he outranked them, they were implemented anyway. Sometimes, but not often, a disgruntled man would shoot daggers at his back with his eyes. Then things would return to normal and all would go on as before.

This was different. He knew now what his wife meant when she tried to explain to him how she felt, but once again, he did not even try to understand. He continued to walk toward the house and the feeling left him. Just as he reached the patio door, the police stepped out. Detective Chin was following close behind them.

"Mr. Kelley, what do you think you were doing? You do realize you could have been killed by taking off like that." Detective Chin said angrily.

"I know, I know. My wife said the same thing. I was so afraid he would get away that I guess I wasn't thinking straight." Angry at himself for what he had done made Seth's face red.

"He had a car waiting on that old dirt road over that way," Seth said as he pointed in the direction he came from.

"I guess that was probably what he was counting on in case somebody did spot him. It's always good to have an exit plan," said Detective Chin. He made a motion for the officer standing there to check the area Seth had just left.

As the officer walked off in the direction Seth pointed, he took two other policemen with him. They searched the area from the house to the road, but didn't find anything.

As Seth watched the policemen search, he turned to Detective Chin saying, "Detective, I had the strangest thing happen to me after I lost John Bledsoe. I turned around and headed back toward the house and the hairs on the back of my neck stood up. I had the distinct feeling someone was watching me, which seems very strange since I had just chased the man that was watching the house away."

Detective Bonner arrived and joined them on the back patio.

"Sorry I couldn't answer your call. I heard it when it came in, but my wife and I were on our way to the emergency room with our son."

"Kids never cease to amaze me. My son was playing baseball all afternoon with a group of kids. However, he ignored the fact that he was sick to his stomach and his side hurt. They continued to play until they couldn't see the ball anymore. Then he came home. After watching T.V for a little while, he said he didn't feel very good and went to bed. Later on, he woke up complaining his side hurt really bad and he then started throwing up. Your call came just as we were leaving the house. Sorry! I take it Detective Chin was able to help you."

"Yes, everyone got here as fast as they could. It just wasn't fast enough. He got away. I ran after him, but I tripped on a root, fell, and lost him. He had a car hidden and when I reached the road all I saw was his tail lights."

"Mr. Kelley, you do realize how incredibly stupid that was?"

"Detective Bonner, could I speak to you for a moment?" Detective Chin said as he motioned him to follow him a short distance away so they could talk and not be heard.

Seth and Chloe looked at each other. Seth held out his arms and Chloe went into them seeking the comfort they always provided. They stood there holding on to each other as they watched the detectives talk. As Seth held her, she said a silent prayer thanking God for her husband's safety.

"You're praying aren't you?" Seth said as he pushed her away from him looking into her tear-filled eyes.

"You do realize I could have lost you when you went off into the woods like that?" Chloe said quietly. "I was just thanking God for taking care of you."

Detective Bonner decided it was necessary for the police to retrace their steps to make sure there wasn't anything there they could have missed. Though the police were none too happy they did what the Detective wanted. A short time later, the police officer returned and headed toward the detectives. The other policemen returned to their vehicles with two different paper bags in hand.

The officer started speaking as he approached the detectives, "We found a couple of suspicious items, but that was all. Some tire marks on the dirt road, but I don't know if they'll be of much help because there were quite a few and we couldn't tell which ones belonged to the suspect. If that's all you need, I'll go ahead and return to the station?"

"I think that's it for now. Thanks for your help."

"No problem, sir," the police officer said as he walked toward the police cruiser.

47

The detectives returned to talk to Seth Kelley.

"Mr. Kelley, please tell me we don't need to caution you about going off on your own to try and catch Mr. Bledsoe, or whoever is trying to kill your wife," Detective Bonner repeated once again. "It does not help your wife, nor does it help us." Both detectives turned and walked around the house and got into their own vehicles and left.

☙

He returned to the woods and concealed himself in its darkness. Once again he was watching the woman. He would get her. It was just a matter of time. He was a patient man.

☙

Seth and Chloe walked inside the house at the same time the detectives were returning to their cars. They both had the feeling that this situation was far from being over, but they also knew that no matter what happened God was with them.

Chapter Fourteen

T he man watched as he smiled to himself. He picked a nice big tree, leaned up against it, and stood staring at the house waiting to see if she would come out or not.

Every time he came close to being able to finish his job something out of the ordinary took place. Now he needed a diversion. He needed something to take the police's attention away from this house for just a little while.

ର

Chloe was in the kitchen. She was not sure what she wanted to do, but she hated having all the curtains closed. She loved being outside and when she couldn't be outside, she decorated the house so the inside would feel like the outside. She put plants all around and opened the curtains as far as they would go; but now she was a prisoner in her own home.

Seth was once again talking to his boss explaining why he needed to take a leave of absence at this time.

Seth and his boss, Calvin, had been friends for a long time and had worked together on several projects that required them to be away from home for long periods of time. Because of that friendship, Calvin was bending over backwards to help Seth anyway that he could.

Even though Calvin could use his help right now, he knew Chloe needed him more. After discussing the ins and outs of how Seth could help with the different problems at the company and at the same time be there for his wife, they finally came up with an answer that seemed good for everyone; at least for the time being.

The plan was for Seth to go to work on Monday and Friday and bring Chloe with him. She could either stay at the office or go shopping; whatever she wanted to do. Then he would work from home Tuesday, Wednesday, and Thursday. It was inconvenient for everyone, but right now it was the only plan they had.

ॐ

John Bledsoe was sorry he had taken this job. Nothing had gone right from the very beginning and now the police were keeping an eye on him. They had arrested him the other night, but they had to let him go because they didn't have enough evidence to keep him. However, they did have enough for them to keep an eye on him.

He didn't understand how they could have found anything because he had been very thorough when he cleaned the woods behind the Kelley's house. He wondered how they found anything that pointed to him, but he knew they had.

He stayed away from the Kelley's the last couple of days to let things die down. He knew the police could not keep an eye on him twenty-four seven for any extended period of time, so he simply waited. He wanted this job to be over and done with so he could get back to his own life. It may not be the best life, but it was his life, and he wanted it back.

Pressure was building inside and out. He needed to follow through. He needed to finish this job. He needed to kill "the woman".

ॐ

Once again it was Monday morning and Chloe was going to Houston with her husband. She was already tired of driving back and forth sitting in her husband's office, or shopping. She had never thought she would be tired of shopping, but boy was she wrong.

"What to do today?" She couldn't think of one thing. She knew she didn't want to be here. She wanted to be home in her own house, doing her own thing. She really appreciated Calvin helping them with their problem as much as he had, but she didn't want to be here anymore.

Chloe hated doing housework, but right now she would love to be home doing housework or swimming. She loved to swim and missed it when she didn't get to. She had lost so much since this man had decided to stalk her. She not only felt like a prisoner in her own home; she felt like a prisoner away from home. She wasn't the master of her own fate anymore; someone else was and she was getting really tired of it.

Today Chloe brought a book with her to the office just in case she couldn't decide what else she wanted to do. Seth and Calvin fixed her a little reading area in the conference room where at least she didn't feel like she was getting in everybody's way. It gave her some semblance of privacy; until it was needed for a meeting.

She sat down, picked up her book and started to read. As hard as she tried, she couldn't keep her mind on what she was reading. She kept trying to think of a way to get Seth to let her stay home instead of coming to the office. So far she could not think of one.

She could hardly wait for the middle of the week so they would be able to stay home. She knew that going to Houston two days a week wasn't very bad, but week after week loomed ahead and she didn't want to do it.

When Seth was home, he would go out by the swimming pool while she swam. He would take his laptop so she could swim as long as she wanted to. She appreciated it, but she never had any alone time. She guessed this was probably as close to her old life as she was going to get until John Bledsoe was caught.

During the past couple of weeks or so, Chloe had not felt any discomfort when she was swimming or even while she was sitting on the patio. She had talked to Detective Bonner, but he told her she needed to stay on the alert anyway. John Bledsoe may have disappeared for the moment and they may not know where he was right now, but he was still out there. As far as they could tell, she was still his target.

The police were keeping an eye out for him, but they were not going on a manhunt for him. So she needed to be aware of her surroundings at all times. Detective Bonner tried to drill that into her head every time he saw her.

"No, no, no," thought Chloe as she sat in her chair trying to figure out how to get her life back.

Chapter Fifteen

The man was once again in the woods behind the house. He had free reign of the whole area on Monday and Fridays because, as far as he could tell Chloe went to work with her husband.

He had even gone swimming in their swimming pool. Being that close and actually swimming where she swam gave him a thrill. He knew he could get caught, but at that moment, it was worth it.

The house was secluded because it was set back off the road, so the probability of him getting caught wasn't very good. While Seth and Chloe were gone, he walked around as much as he could trying to formulate some kind of a plan. He passed the pool and felt the urge to get in, knowing he shouldn't. He decided to do it anyway.

As he swam, he pictured Chloe as she swam. Being there gave him a feeling of empowerment and he enjoyed the feeling. He knew he would have to leave soon, but he was going to enjoy it as long as he could.

When he stopped swimming, he heard the sirens in the distance. He didn't know if the sirens were meant for him or not, but he decided it was time to leave. He jumped out of the pool by going over the side instead of using the ladder. Because he didn't use the ladder he did not see his watch laying on one of the steps; so he left it.

As he got to the edge of the woods, he remembered putting his watch on the ladder so that it would not get wet, but by then it was too late. The police cars were driving up to the house. Someone must have called them, because when they got out of their cars, they didn't go to the front door. They went straight to the pool area. Some raced to search the area around the pool and some went immediately into the woods. When they heard a car take off in the distance, they knew they were too late.

☙

Detective Bonner was angry with himself, because he had not sent a police car to the entrance of the dirt road. He knew that was the only way in or out. If he had just been thinking; but he hadn't. Now they had lost John Bledsoe once again, and it was up to him to inform the Kelley's as to what had taken place.

He took his cell phone out to make the call when one of the policemen came up to him with a bag in his hand. In the bag was a watch. The policeman informed him it had been found on one of the ladder steps.

He felt a little better about calling the Kelley's. He knew there was no excuse for losing John Bledsoe, but if the watch on the ladder was not Mr. Kelley's they would have proof positive that Mr. Bledsoe was in an area he had no business being in.

Seth sat quietly as he heard what Detective Bonner had to say. Once he was through talking he went to Calvin's office. He had to talk to someone as a friend, not as a boss.

Chapter Sixteen

C hloe read the same page several times, but still did not know what it said. As she started over one more time, Seth and Calvin came into the room. Seth pulled a couple of chairs out from under the table and placed them both in front of her.

Calvin sat there quietly as Seth started to speak.

"Chloe, we think we have come up with a solution to our situation; at least for a little while. Calvin has a job that needs some help on an island northwest of Australia and it could last anywhere from three to six months. What do you think about just picking up and making a temporary move?"

"The house is already there and it is furnished. There are still a few things that need to be worked out, but we should know one way or the other by Friday."

"If everything turns out like we hope it will, we will start packing our suitcases and bring them to the office each Monday and Friday until we leave. Then what we have not had time to bring, we will just buy when we get to Australia before we go to the island. We will be gone ever how long the job takes. I know it's not a permanent solution, but it will give us a breather. What do you think?" Seth asked as he waited for Chloe's answer.

Chloe sat there for all of three seconds. She jumped up and hugged her husband and then she hugged Calvin.

"I think that is just about the greatest idea I have ever heard.

Let's go home and start packing. I am ready to leave right this minute."

Seth and Calvin both laughed and left the room as their conversation immediately returned to the job.

Chloe sat there as she watched them leave. Her first thought was that she was going to get her freedom back if only for a little while. The second thought went to thinking about what she needed to pack. She knew the final day would need to look as if they were simply going away for the weekend.

She saw a pad of paper sitting on the conference room table with a pencil lying beside it. She went over, picked it up and returned to her chair with a smile covering her face from ear to ear. Her whole body breathed a sigh of relief and happiness spread over her whole demeanor.

Her only problem now as she started making her list was she and her husband could not leave fast enough.

Chapter Seventeen

Today was the day. It had taken longer than they expected, but now they were ready to go. They pulled their car out of the garage so it would look like they were just going away for the weekend in case John Bledsoe was watching.

Seth and Chloe had been able to fill several footlockers until each one had no more room available. They would take them to Seth's office. The footlockers would be forwarded to the island where they were going just before they were ready to leave. They were both so elated at leaving; it was hard not to jump for joy at the thought that this would be their last day in the States for a while. They loved their home. They loved their country, but they needed a break.

Seth called Detective Bonner from his office on Monday to let him know they were going to be out of the country. He agreed that it was a great idea and told them both to have a good time and to fully enjoy their respite.

Chloe called Darla on the one side of their property and Connie on the other side to let them know they were going to be gone for a while. She asked the both of them to keep an eye on their home for them.

She also called relatives and friends from the office to let them know that they were going to be out of the country; but she did not tell them the real reason behind the decision to go. Seth was the one that actually advised both Darla and Connie as to what was and what had been going on. He had given Darla the keys to the house in case she needed them. He had also given her some money to buy pool supplies, if and when they were needed.

The suitcases were ready and sitting by the front door. Each one took turns making one last sweep through the house to make sure they had not left anything. Though, even if she had, at this point Chloe didn't care. She just wanted to be gone.

Instead of going to the office this morning, Seth and Chloe were going straight to Bush Intercontinental Airport. The closer they got to the airport the more relaxed they began to feel. They were taking Continental from Houston to Hawaii. They were going to spend a week there just relaxing. From there, it would be time to go to Australia and then travel to the island where they would be staying.

Seth and Calvin went to great lengths to make sure there would be no complications on this trip. Security wise they planned their departure down to the time the plane took off.

They decided to park the company car in one of the parking garages along the road leading up to Bush Intercontinental. This part of the plan had not been pre-arranged for security reasons. On the day of departure, Seth would decide where he wanted to park. Since the police did not know where John Bledsoe was, they were being extra cautious.

Seth would put the parking ticket in an envelope and then put it in the mail before they went through the security area of the airport. Once Calvin received the ticket, he would go get the car. It seemed like an awful lot to go through just to go overseas, but for Chloe's safety it was necessary.

Seth and Chloe took Highway 59, South until they got to Humble. Once on the south side of Humble they took Will Clayton exit and headed toward the airport.

Seth followed the "International Departure" signs. He pulled up in front of Departures and let Chloe out. He then went to the back of the car and got the suitcases out of the trunk. They only had two small ones a piece because the others had been sent on ahead. Before Chloe took the suitcases Seth said, "Chloe, I want you to find a place to sit down that has a lot of people around you. You're going to be alone while I go park the car. I want you to please be careful. We don't know anything about this man, nor do we know how much he knows about us. So remember Detective Bonner's advice and be aware of your surroundings at all times."

Seth handed her the tickets and then watched as she entered through the automatic glass doors. He then got into his company car and drove to a parking garage located on the road approaching the airport. After parking, he waited for the shuttle bus to pick him up. While he waited, Seth went ahead and put the parking ticket into a pre-addressed envelope to Calvin. He would mail it as soon as he found a mailbox.

The shuttle bus approached and as he got on, he breathed a sigh of relief. They were actually only hours away from finally being safe. He got off the shuttle as it reached his destination and he went through the same automated glass doors as Chloe had and now he looked around to see if he could find her.

She was sitting in an area that was very crowded. He smiled because she didn't always do what he wanted her to do, but thankfully this time she had. He watched her for just a minute and hoped that going overseas was the right decision. As he watched, Chloe's cell phone rang. She answered and turned white as a sheet.

"Where are you going?" the voice said.

"What do you mean?"

"I said. Where are you going? Do you really think you can get away from me?"

Seth reached her side at that moment and she held out her phone to him. When he put the phone to his ear, he said, "Whoever you are I want you to leave my wife alone. Do you hear me?"

The voice on the other end laughed and then hung up. Both Seth and Chloe looked at each other in silence; neither one knowing what to say or do.

Finally Seth said, "Let's go ahead and go through security. That will at least limit the amount of people around us. Then I guess we should probably call Detective Bonner and tell him what happened and see what he thinks."

Once they got their luggage checked through they both started toward the security gate watching as they went to see if anyone was following them.

Both Chloe and Seth thought taking this job was the answer to their problem, but now they weren't for sure. As they went through security and walked on down to their boarding gate, they were both sinking deep into their own thoughts. Chloe was about to cry and Seth was very angry. How dare this man, this man they did not even know, mess up their lives so completely.

They stopped at their gate area and picked out some seats where they could sit down together. As Chloe sat down, Seth moved off to the side so he would be in an area where he would not be overheard by the other passengers. He pulled out his cell phone and pressed the number he had for Detective Bonner and then proceeded to fill him in on what had just happened.

Since Detective Bonner already knew about their moving, that wasn't a surprise, but John Bledsoe calling Chloe's cell phone did concern him. He didn't know how he would have gotten her phone number.

"I think before we make any assumptions about anything I probably need to go and check out your house. Then we'll go from there."

"Our next door neighbor, Darla, has the key to the house. If you decide you need to get in, we have already informed her you might need it. So all you have to do is go ask her. Please let me know as soon as you find out anything. I really want to know what is going on."

"Will do," said Detective Bonner. "I will contact you as soon as I know something. If you're busy, I will leave you a voice mail; or better yet I'll call your office." All of this was said on the slight chance that somehow their cell phones had been bugged. At this point, they just couldn't be too careful.

The company gave Seth a cell phone to be used for business only, but they allowed Seth to get an accompanying one for Chloe's personal use. Usually this wouldn't be done, but there were extenuating circumstances and a strong friendship between Seth and Calvin, and their families. Their personal phones would be turned off as soon as they boarded their plane. They would not even use these phones for the whole period of time they were gone.

Chapter Eighteen

The man stood in the woods like he had so many times before. He watched as the Kelley's put their suitcases in Seth's company car, and he wondered how long they would be gone this time. Since they were only taking two suitcases, he assumed they were probably going away for the weekend.

He found other hiding places on both sides of the house so now he did not have to solely rely on the woods to keep him concealed. Sometimes he liked it when they were gone for the weekend. It almost gave him free reign to do and to see what he wanted just like he was doing right now. He entered their house not long after they left, going from room to room and pretending it was his. He wondered if they had ever felt his presence after being gone for the day. He loved being in their house and pretending that Chloe was his. When it happened, he didn't know, but somewhere along the way this job had changed. He wanted Chloe for himself. He was no longer doing it for "the man". Of course, he hadn't told him yet.

When it was time to leave, he pretended he had killed her because of her unfaithfulness. She belonged to him! Not Seth!! Not "the man"!! How was he ever going to find someone who was faithful?"

He had fulfilled his fantasy for the day and was getting ready to leave when he saw someone pulling into the drive. He wondered who it could be. Since the Kelley's were gone, he thought he was safe being in their house.

He ran to the patio door, went out, and locked the glass door behind him. He ran to the edge of the woods and then slipped into the darkness beyond. As soon as he was hidden by the surrounding foliage, he stopped and turned to see if anyone would come to the back of the house. Silently he waited. As a man came around the side of the house, he was pretty sure he was the detective that had been there before. He wondered why he was here.

He continued to watch as the detective looked through the patio door. The Kelley's had only partially pulled the curtains shut so it was easy to look into the house. The man watched as the detective pulled at the patio door to make sure it was locked. When he found it was, he continued on around the house.

The man stayed put just listening. He didn't want to leave his hiding place, but he needed to make sure he was there alone. In a few moments he heard the car door slam, the engine started, and then slowly he could hear the car getting farther and farther away until he could hear the engine no more. He made his way to the front of the house and checked to make sure the car was gone. It was and he returned to the safety of the woods once again wondering why the detective had been here.

⚃

Once he got the call from Seth, Detective Bonner decided to drive by their house. He had not been far away when he had received Seth's call, so it was just a matter of minutes before he arrived in front of their house.

As he got out of the car, his eyes immediately started looking for something out of place. He walked around the house but everything seemed to be in place. So, he returned to his car and continued on his way to the police station.

⚃

"Continental Flight___, for Honolulu, Hawaii now boarding at Gate___," said the voice over the loud speaker system.

Seth and Chloe got up and thankfully headed toward the door through which they would board the plane. They joined the other passengers in line, continually checking everyone around them. They checked the passengers already in line, and those starting to get in line as their row was called.

As they found their seats and sat down, they both felt a sense of relief spread through their bodies. Chloe silently said, "Thank you Lord for this respite. No matter how short it is. I thank you."

Seth and Chloe began to talk as they waited for all the passengers to get to their seats and for the plane to actually take off. When it did, Chloe leaned over and gave her husband a kiss.

"I love you, Seth," she said. "And I am so looking forward to living on an island in the South Pacific for a while."

"I love you, too Chloe, and I am actually looking forward to it too."

After they talked for a while, Seth took out his company computer so he could get some work done en route. Thankfully, the company had bought them first class tickets, which gave him plenty of room to work without being cramped.

When they first found their seats, Chloe tried to settle in with a good book, but she found that as each passenger passed by her chair, she would look up to check them out. She was just being on the safe side. She looked at Seth and he was doing the same thing. Now the plane was in the air and she could relax and read because they were on their way to a brand new life, at least for a little while. If anything came up that needed to be taken care of, Darla had Calvin's number. She also had Detective Bonner's cell phone number. Hopefully, all the bases were covered.

 C3

The man returned Monday, Tuesday, and Wednesday thinking they would have returned by then, but since they hadn't, he decided maybe they were going to be gone for the week. He left deciding he would come back the following Monday to see if they were back yet.

ᝄ

He arrived bright and early and sat waiting for Chloe to come out and go swimming. He waited, but she didn't show up. He walked up to the back patio and sat down. He wondered where she was and why she had been gone so long.

As he sat there, he decided maybe they had taken a two-week vacation. He didn't like it, but there was nothing he could do about it. He didn't like it at all. He got up and retreated back into the woods. He didn't even feel like breaking into their house; he was so upset. He walked back to his car and drove away.

Chapter Nineteen

eth and Chloe finally landed in Australia. The company representative met them at the airport. After retrieving their suitcases, he took them to a hotel telling them he would be back early the next morning to pick them up to start them on the last leg of their journey.

They both slept soundly and were thankful they had put in for a wakeup call of 5:00 a.m. They were dressed and ready when the driver showed up at 6:00 a.m. to return them to the airport.

There they, and several other new employees, boarded the company plane for a mining town on the island of Papua New Guinea. This is where Seth and Chloe would spend the next several months.

After arriving on the island, they boarded a helicopter that would take them to the town where they would be living. Each family was taken to the house they would occupy while they were employed there. The trip had been long and even though they had stayed over in Hawaii for a week, by the time they walked through the doors of their new house they were wiped out.

There was food already in the house when they got there. The town had a welcoming committee and they made sure each new family had enough food to tide them over until they could make a trip to the company store.

Seth and Chloe sat and talked for a short while and then decided to turn in early. Seth would start his new job the next day and some of the ladies of the town would come by to meet Chloe and so their new life would begin.

Seth had already left by the time Chloe got up. She made some coffee and rehashed the events that had brought them to this island. She marveled at the way so many things had just fit into place. They needed somewhere to just get away, then out of the blue this job made itself known. This is what Chloe called a "God Thing."

A friend of Calvin's needed help. She didn't know exactly what it was that Seth was going to do, but it didn't matter. At the same time this friend needed help, she and Seth were under a lot of stress and this seemed to be the perfect solution. Only time would tell.

೮౩

The man continued to watch the house and everyday Seth and Chloe didn't come home the angrier he became. Things were just not going the way he had planned.

How had they gotten out of the house without him knowing? Then he remembered he had even watched them go, but he had thought they were going on vacation; not that he could have done anything about it. That made him even angrier. What to do? What to do?

He decided to go into the house again. He had done that same thing right after their supposed long weekend and he had found the cell phone number on the refrigerator door. He called the number and asked her where she was going. Maybe he should do it again.

The man left the safety of the woods after he had stood there making sure he was alone. He walked up to the back patio door, but remembered he had locked it when the detective had shown up. Then he slowly moved around to the front door and picked the lock. He walked in and looked around the room.

He went into the living room and sat down. The house had an

empty feel to it now. Not like the other times he had been there. He sat for a while trying to come up with a plan. His mind drew a blank. He got up and went over to the refrigerator. The number was still there, so he turned to the phone and picked it up. He checked to see if there was a dial tone, and yes there was. He dialed the number he had taken off the refrigerator door, and there was no signal. It was dead. He threw the phone across the room. They had really planned this out and he had been none the wiser.

○ঽ

Seth and Chloe settled into their new life very quickly. They both made friends and became active in the community.

The only way they were able to communicate with family and friends was either by writing letters or by a telegram from the home office. They were very isolated; and they liked it that way.

They had been on the island for several weeks when they received a telegram from Detective Bonner stating that John Bledsoe had been found dead in his room from a drug overdose. The telegram was worded in a way where no one but the intended party would know what it really said.

Detective Bonner was not one hundred percent sure John Bledsoe was the one that was giving Chloe problems, so even though they were relieved, there was still a question lurking in the back of their minds. When he was arrested the first time, he told the police someone had hired him. Detective Bonner could not eliminate that possibility all together.

○ঽ

Killing John Bledsoe had only slightly assuaged his anger. Now he again started to check the house day by day for movement. If John Bledsoe had done his job in the first place then--------------. Oh well, there was nothing he could do about that now.

68

He returned to the woods behind the house. It was quiet!! Very quiet. He stood there and watched, but he didn't see anyone. So he went into house through the front door. This time, when he left, he would leave the patio door open and lock the front door. Watching John Bledsoe as he had watched Chloe had not only been entertaining but it was also educational.

After getting into the house, he went from room to room. He liked being in her house and touching her things. He wanted her here and he wanted her here now.

Chapter Twenty

Seth's troubleshooting job was coming to an end. There were only a few more days left, and they would be going home. In fact, their clothes and other personal belongings had already been sent on ahead. They had only kept the bare essentials with them and they were going to stay in the VIP apartment. They would eat in the restaurant until the time they left. The other basic needs came with the apartment.

They had made some good friends while they were there, but Chloe knew it was time to go home. She was glad they were going back, but at the same time her fear was returning. Time was passing faster and faster and her fear was returning at the same rate.

Instead of going straight home, they were going to fly from Cairns, Queensland to Sydney. They had decided they would stay in Sydney a few days sight-seeing and then they would fly to Los Angeles and stop to visit her sister. She had not told her sister anything about the problem she was having. She knew her sister would be mad, but there really was nothing she could have done, and life was too short to be mad for a long time.

Seth and Chloe spent a few days with her sister catching up on old times, going shopping, and taking part in some of the tourist activities found around the town, but then they both decided it was time to go home. So the next day they took a flight to Houston.

Calvin met them at the airport, and then he took them to the office.

From Seth's office phone, he called Detective Bonner. He wanted more information than what the telegram had been able to tell him. Detective Bonner was out of the office so he called his cell phone, which is what he should have done in the first place.

"Detective Bonner," the detective said as he answered his cell phone.

"Detective Bonner, this is Seth Kelley. I was wondering if I could speak with you for a minute. My wife and I are back in the States and I need to know how safe it is for us to go home."

"Mr. Kelley, I know you know that John Bledsoe is dead. His death was apparently a drug overdose, but something just doesn't seem right to me."

"I don't know what to tell you about going home. A patrol car does go by every once in a while. You don't live very close to town, so it's not done very often. They have never reported any suspicious activity and neither have any of your neighbors."

"I have some business out that way to attend to. Since I am headed in that direction anyway, I can go check it out for you if you would like."

"Actually, Detective Bonner, I think I would like that and I know that my wife would. Ever since we landed, I can see the fear returning in her eyes. I guess it's not only her, but me too. I'll wait for you to call me back. Thanks a lot." Seth said quietly into the phone.

Seth went ahead and gave Calvin an update on all that had taken place in the mining town while he waited for Detective Bonner to call him back. He would write an official report later. He just couldn't seem to keep his mind on business right now.

Thankfully, Calvin understood his frame of mind and told him he could send his report in later once he and Chloe returned home and had rested up a little.

Chloe sat in the conference room as she had so many months before. She felt the old fear returning. "Oh, God! I thought I had a handle on the way I feel, but I don't. I'm afraid. Please, Lord help me!"

Seth came in while Chloe was praying and joined in. He simply took her hand in agreement. They both knew that the Bible said, *"where any two are gathered together in His name that there He is also."* God had seen them through this far, and they trusted Him to see them through to the end. No matter what the end turned out to be.

Calvin brought Seth's company car to the office and he parked it in the company's parking lot. He gave Seth the keys. Seth and Chloe grabbed their suitcases and headed for the car. While Seth was putting the suitcases in the trunk, Detective Bonner called.

"Mr. Kelley?"

"Yes, Detective. Did you have a chance to check out the house?"

"Yes, I did. It seems okay. I didn't find anything out of place on the outside, but I did not go on the inside. Everything seems to be okay. I do want to caution you, and whether you tell your wife this or not is up to you. We are not one-hundred percent sure John Bledsoe was the stalker. Everything pointed to him, but it seemed just a little too pat for me."

"Thanks, Detective. I guess we will head for home then. We really appreciate all you've done."

"You're welcome, Mr. Kelley. I wish I could have done more. Hopefully we will not meet again, but if you need my help, do not hesitate to call."

Seth brought their conversation to an end, and then went around and opened the door on the passenger side of the car for Chloe. She slipped into the seat and Seth shut the door. They were now on their way home. Excitement and fear were intermingled in their thoughts as they headed out on the freeway. It took them about three hours to get home. Rush hour traffic had been horrific, but now they were driving up in front of the house and it felt so good to be home.

They had called Darla and Connie to let them know they were there. It was nice to have neighbors that would keep an eye on everything while you were gone, whether it was for a couple of weeks or for several months, but now they were back.

They pulled into the garage and let the door come down behind them. Deciding to leave everything until tomorrow morning they simply went in and sat down in their recliners, and relaxed. They turned the T.V. on, but neither one of them was really watching it.

It was so good to be home. Chloe asked Seth if he thought he would like a cup of coffee, but thinking it might keep him awake he decided he would wait until the following morning. Since Seth didn't want any coffee, Chloe decided she would wait too. She went ahead and went into the bedroom to put her nightgown on.

Once ready for bed she returned to the living room and sat down beside Seth; both just enjoying being together and being home. Tomorrow was Saturday so neither one of them had to get up early. Chloe had thought about going for a swim, but she was just too tired. She didn't think she could muster up the strength to climb up the ladder. It was just one more thing that would have to wait until tomorrow.

&#x3;

The next morning Seth and Chloe got up late, and after eating brunch, they decided to unpack. So they brought their suitcases in the house. Not really wanting to mess with unpacking they decided to go to the grocery store first. Plus, they needed to check on pool supplies and for that they would have to go to Darla's. While they were there they could find out what had been taking place in the neighborhood.

Each made a list as to what they thought they might need. Chloe called Darla to see if she was going to be home so they could stop by on their way to town. She was also heading in that direction, but agreed to wait for them. Since they hadn't seen each other for quite a while, they talked a lot longer than what they should have and it was later in the day before they finally got started on their individual errands.

Darla walked them to their car but before they could drive off she told Chloe she needed to ask her one more question.

"I don't want to spook you or anything. I know about all the stuff that was happening before you left, but I got to where every time I checked on, or worked on the pool I felt as if someone was watching me. It got so bad I started taking someone with me all the time. I thought the man who had been stalking you was dead. Anyway, I just thought I should let you know. Talk to you later."

As Seth and Chloe got into their car, Chloe turned to Seth and asked him, "Seth, what do you think?"

"I don't know what to think. With John Bledsoe dead, I thought we had put all that stuff behind us. Now, I guess when we get back from town, we better check in with Detective Bonner. We should probably talk to him while we're in town, but I just don't want to. Let's play it by ear. If we do, we do. If we don't, we don't."

Seth and Chloe got their shopping done, as soon as possible, and returned home. After they had put everything up, Seth went to call the detective. He went to the counter, but the phone wasn't there. He looked around and found it on the floor. He didn't remember seeing it there last night, but they had been tired and hadn't needed to call anyone.

"Chloe, did you drop the phone?"

"No I didn't. Why? Where is it?"

"It's lying on the floor. I guess we could have knocked it off the counter when we got ready to leave and didn't realize it. It just seems like it would have made enough noise that we would have noticed. I guess we can use our cell phones. It just seems a little strange that's all."

"I didn't really want to use our cell phones yet." Chloe said, staring at the phone, as Seth bent over to pick it up off of the floor.

"After I got the call when we were in the airport, it really scared me and now I am a little afraid to start using it again. I guess we have to do it sooner or later, but I would just as soon do it later."

"Why don't we go over to Connie's and let her know we are home. While we're there I'll ask if I can use her phone and I'll call Detective Bonner. This way I can let him know we are actually home, let Connie know we are home, and at the same time let him know that something doesn't seem right."

"After church tomorrow, we'll run into town and pick up a new phone. It should work without any problem since we didn't have the phone turned off before we left."

"We turned the cell phones in that we used while we were gone because they were the company's and are used only for those men going overseas. Otherwise, I could use that one to call."

They were enjoying a short visit with Connie when Seth asked if he could use the phone. When Connie said yes, he excused himself and went into the other room so he could talk privately to Detective Bonner. Detective Bonner could not tell him much more than he already had; which did not make Seth feel any better. Once again, he was at a loss as to what to do. So he hung up and returned to the living room where the girls were still talking.

"Chloe, we probably need to get on our way. Why don't we go ahead and go get us a phone now. Then we won't have to do anything after church if we don't want to."

Chloe said her goodbyes. She could tell that Seth wasn't too happy.

"What happened with Detective Bonner?"

"Not much. He didn't have any more information than he gave me before. Since I don't have anything concrete to give him and John Bledsoe is dead, he's at a loss of what to do. He will come take a look in the woods if we want him to, but I told him I would get back with him on that."

"I know you didn't believe me in the beginning, but I really appreciate all you're doing now. I don't know whether you believe Darla or not and since John Bledsoe is dead it's hard for me too. But at the same time I know how I felt so I cannot dismiss the way she feels. It's all so very confusing."

Seth and Chloe went back to town and got a phone. While they were there, they went ahead and went out to eat. They just relaxed and talked. They made sure their conversation did not contain anything about John Bledsoe, his death, the weird thing with the phone, or with Darla's feelings while taking care of the pool.

After they ate, they decided to head for home. Chloe decided she wanted to go for a swim. So Seth decided he would take his laptop out to the pool so he could keep an eye on her.

"I guess I'm just a really big coward because I'm still afraid to go swim. Even knowing that man is dead I don't want to go. I hate that. I hate that someone can make me feel this way, and that someone is dead. I hate it that I need you to watch me, because it makes me feel like I can't take care of myself; and I can't because that man almost drowned me. Weird, huh?"

Once they go home, Chloe decided she wasn't ready to go swimming so she snuggled up in front of the T.V. while Seth got out his computer and worked sitting at the kitchen table. When he finished what he needed to do, he went over and sat by Chloe. She snuggled in his arms and they both sat watching T.V. deep in their own thoughts. There they sat and that's where they were when they fell asleep, and they stayed asleep well into the night.

Chapter Twenty-One

C hloe woke with a start. She laid there for several minutes trying to figure out what had caused her to wake up. She raised herself up off the recliner so she could look out the patio door. They had both fallen asleep in the living room as they were watching T.V. so the back patio curtains were still open.

A movement on the patio caught her attention and she froze. She knew animals came up on the patio all the time, and some were little and some were big. But somehow, she didn't think this shadow was an animal's.

Did she dare get up and look out the patio door? She didn't think she was brave enough, so she just laid there hoping Seth would wake up. There was no noise coming from the inside or outside of the house. She was afraid to move because if someone was out there, she was afraid they would see her.

Was that a movement? Was that a sound? "Seth, wake up!" She was afraid to shove him to wake him up because he always woke up with such a start. Depending on how deep he was asleep he could also make a lot of noise, and she didn't want to take a chance on that. "Seth, wake up!" she said as loud as she could but not loud enough that if someone was outside, they would be able to hear her, but loud enough so Seth would hear her; but he didn't budge.

Since the house was in complete darkness, she decided she would try to get up without making a lot of noise. Slowly she moved away from Seth, never letting her eyes move away from the patio door. Luckily, she had been lying in his arms when they went to sleep, which made it easier for her to slip away from him.

Was that a shadow? She stared at the door hardly daring to breathe. When she finally made it off the recliner, she moved toward the door.

As Chloe stepped in front of the patio door, someone stepped in front of her. When the door opened and she and the intruder came face to face, he could not contain his surprise. They stared at each other for what seemed like an eternity, but in reality was only a few seconds. Then he turned around running toward the woods. When he stumbled over a chair, he grabbed it all the while never losing his balance. He threw it out of his way as he started running toward the woods.

When Chloe saw him, she screamed, more from surprise than fear. Fear kicked in very quickly and though she didn't run she did back up as fast as she could. As she backed up, her knees came in contact with a kitchen chair and she stopped.

When Seth heard her scream, he jumped up off the recliner in complete confusion. It took him a moment to get his bearings and to realize they were in the living room and not in their bedroom. His eyes searched the room for Chloe for several moments before he was able to see her.

She was looking toward the woods and it took him three steps to get to her side. He put his arms around her and asked her what had happened. She turned around and looked at him as she explained what she had just seen. As they stood there, they heard sirens in the distance. The longer they stood there and listened the closer the sirens seemed to be getting. They knew they had not called the police so they wondered what was going on.

As they stood in their front yard, they saw the police cars pass Connie's house and then their mailbox. They continued to watch so they could see where they were going and they were surprised when they saw them turn onto Darla's drive.

They waited for a little while and decided to drive over to Darla's to see what was going on. They were already dressed because they had fallen asleep on the recliner. Seth grabbed his keys as he and Chloe went and got in the car. They backed out of the garage and closed the door behind them. At first the police were not going to let them pass so they could go up to the house, but as they told them what had just happened to them, they let them by.

One of the policemen showed Seth and Chloe to where Detective Bonner and Darla were seated. Chloe went straight to Darla to see if she was alright. Not knowing why Darla had called the police, she was concerned.

Seth went to Detective Bonner and relayed their story, which had only happened a few minutes ago. When the detective heard what Seth had to say, he asked all three of them to sit down so they could see if they could put all the puzzle pieces together, or if by chance they were completely different circumstances and the puzzle pieces wouldn't fit. No one gathered in the living room thought that was the case. Was Darla's break-in not even related to what was happening to the Kelley's or was there something they were missing? Were the pieces related and if they were, how?

Darla started at the beginning. She had gone to her daughter's but something came up and her daughter had to go attend to it. At first Darla thought she would go ahead and spend the night anyway, but she decided she would rather go home if her daughter wasn't going to be there.

"It was late when I got back so I pulled into the garage and shut the garage door. When I got into the house, I noticed the patio door was wide open. Knowing that I had locked it before I left, I decided to call you, Detective Bonner."

"I was scared enough that I just turned around and went back to the garage and got back into the car. Then   I backed out and drove down to the mailbox and stayed there until you arrived. You arrived first and shortly thereafter the police. I hadn't put my purse down yet, and my cell phone was in my purse so that was how I was able to call out. I called 911, but then I called Detective Bonner."

Darla looked at Chloe as she was telling her story.

"I knew all about Chloe having trouble with some stalker, but I thought he was dead. So when I came in the house and the door was open, I guess I just freaked out. I got in the car as fast as I could and left."

"Okay Mrs. Bellamy, you've told me what went on here. Seth, Chloe, which one of you wants to tell me what happened up there?"

"Chloe, probably needs to do that. I was asleep until she screamed and everything had already taken place by that time."

"Okay, Mrs. Kelley. What happened?"

Chloe started her story with her and her husband falling asleep on the recliner and she ended with them hearing the sirens and then them driving to Darla's.

"I've actually been trying to make some kind of sense as to what is going on. If John Bledsoe is dead and he's the one that has been causing me a problem, it's a far stretch to think this has anything to do with what has been happening to me. But at the same time when I came face to face with the man on our patio, his face showed complete surprise. I actually think he expected that door to open, but he did not expect me to be there. Why did he expect it to open? He shouldn't have unless he had been in the house before. We haven't used that door since we've been home so it should have been locked." Chloe said as she was looking directly at Detective Bonner. "Why the man broke into Darla's house?" Chloe said as she looked at Seth. "I don't know, but she scared him off when she came home early."

"When Darla scared him off," Chloe said, continuing her train of thought, "he ran up to our house thinking he could get in. Why? I don't know."

"Come to think of it he threw the patio chair after he stumbled over it to get it out of his way. I don't know if he had on gloves, but maybe not. You might check it anyway."

Detective Bonner looked at Darla and said.

"I'm going to place a police car here for the time being. Right now I'm going to the Kelley's to see if I can see anything there, but I want to make sure you are safe while I'm doing that. We can only take one step at a time, and right now this is it. I will let you know what is going on whether I call you or come back to your house. One way or the other you will know something."

The Kelley's and Detective Bonner got into their cars and drove over to the Kelley's house. Seth and Chloe pulled their car into the garage, but with all that was going on they didn't want to leave the garage door open. Chloe went in the house from the garage pushing the garage door closer behind her as she went. Seth waited until the garage door shut and then went around and opened the front door for Detective Bonner.

"Then there is the mystery of the phone. After talking to Darla, and she voiced her concern about feeling as if she was being watched when she went to the house to take care of the pool. We knew we needed to call you, but we were tired and had groceries to get so we put it off."

"After getting everything done, Seth went to get the phone so he could call you and tell you what Darla had told us. It's usually on the kitchen counter, but it wasn't there. We found it on the floor in pieces. When that happened, we don't know. Neither of us can think of when or why that could have happened."

"But with everything going on," Seth said. "I am now convinced that someone has been in our house! Who it was or when it was? We don't know."

Chloe asked both Seth and the detective if they would like a cup of coffee. They didn't answer but she knew she did so she went into the kitchen to make some anyway. She had the distinct feeling it was going to be a long night.

As she was making the coffee, Seth and Detective Bonner passed through the living room and the dining room and went out the patio door. The detective picked up the chair, that whoever had been on the patio threw, and handed it to one of the policemen that had followed him. He used gloves just in case the man had left fingerprints and so did the policeman that took it from him.

"Mrs. Kelley, I really don't want to scare you, but my gut tells me this is your stalker. I don't know how John Bledsoe fit into the picture, but I think he was just the fall guy. This is not official because I don't really have anything to go on but until we find out a little bit more I think you need to stay on high alert."

Detective Bonner got in his car and left. He had the policeman fold the lawn chair and put it into his car. He didn't have a clue how this was going to play out, but he was going to see it through to the end. For now, he would take it to the station and see what forensics could come up with.

Right now he needed some sleep. He didn't even remember what his wife had sent him to the store to get before he got Mrs. Bellamy's call and headed to her house instead of the store. His wife was eight months pregnant and was probably asleep by now and he didn't want to wake her.

He was right. She was asleep, so he went straight to bed and fell asleep just seconds after his head hit his pillow. After a couple hours sleep, he woke up thinking about this case and knew he would not be able to go back to sleep. So he got up, showered, dressed, and got ready to leave for the station. He kissed his wife lightly not wanting to wake her up, then left her a note telling her he loved her and would call her later.

As he drove toward the station, he wondered where this case was headed.

Chapter Twenty-Two

T he man watched everything that was taking place from the safety of the woods behind the Kelley's house. He had picked a big tree with lots of bushes surrounding it. It was the same tree John Bledsoe stood beside while he was watching the woman. He thought it funny that as Bledsoe had watched her, he was watching him.

He didn't think they would search the woods until daylight so he just kept an eye on the policemen patrolling around the house. The curtains were closed, but periodically he would see someone's shadow pass by the window. It would move, then he would be left to wonder who it was and what they were doing.

◌

Detective Bonner left two men patrolling the area while he went home. Seth and Chloe would meet him at the station later. Since she was the one that had seen the man's face through the window, he wanted her to go through some mug shots. If that did not yield anything, maybe she could talk to the police artist and come up with a likeness to the man she had seen. Chloe wasn't sure how that would work because she had only seen his face for such a short period of time. Still she would try and do her best.

Seth and Chloe both took showers and changed into clean clothes. It had been a long night and it looked as if it was going to be a long day. Once they got to the police station the day would no

85

longer be theirs. They needed to do everything in their power to help the police catch this man; not only for Chloe's sake, but for every other woman who lived in and around town.

Instead of fixing breakfast at the house they had decided to stop somewhere along the way. They couldn't decide which would be faster, cooking or stopping to eat; but since Chloe didn't feel like cooking, they decided to eat out.

After arriving at the police station, Detective Bonner's partner set Chloe at a desk with several mug shot books to look through. Someone was nice enough to bring her a cup of coffee and she settled in picking up her first book and opening it to the first page.

Detective Roberts told Seth he could get himself a cup of coffee and sit and wait for Detective Bonner or he could leave and come back later. He informed Seth that he was going to let Detective Bonner know they were there.

They brought Chloe several books, and she went through each and every one of them until the faces all looked the same. It was late afternoon and her stomach was telling her it was time to eat. Detective Bonner and Seth left earlier to do something, but she had been concentrating on what she was doing and had not paid a lot of attention to what was said.

The sketch artist, who introduced herself as Jo Ann, came to the door to see if she was ready to try describing the man she had seen.

"Jo Ann, if you don't mind, I am really hungry. I haven't had anything since breakfast and I thought I would get something to eat before we got started if that's alright with you?" At that point Chloe's stomach growled very loudly.

Jo Ann laughed and said, "I see your point. There is a little soup and sandwich place over on Main Street," and proceeded to tell her exactly where it was located. "I'm sure I can wait long enough for you to eat. Let me know when you get back and we'll get started."

' "If you would tell my husband where I went, I sure would appreciate it." As she spoke, she headed off in the direction of the door and Jo Ann headed off in a different direction.

Chloe left the station and followed Jo Ann's directions. She went in and picked out her soup and sandwich and after paying for it, she went and sat down at a table that was by a window.

She was so deep in thought that at first she forgot to eat. Someone dropped a spoon nearby which brought her back to the present, and as she sat there, once again she began to get the feeling she was being watched. She heard the bell as someone entered the door, and she turned to see who it might be. It turned out to be a little girl and her mother. There was a man and his son jaywalking in front of the store; and that's when she saw him.

He looked at her and smiled and she didn't know what to do. She continued to stare at him and deep down she knew that he was the one. Fear kept her seated; fear kept her looking straight into his eyes. He turned away just as two men decided to cross the street in front of him. She could not hear what was said, but they shook his hand and then turned and crossed the street to where she was eating.

She could not believe her eyes. Her stalker had just shaken hands with both her husband and the detective. Since their backs had been toward her, the man smiled, waved, and walked off down the street.

She could no longer see him so fear no longer had her in its grip. She jumped up and ran to the door; pulling it open just as the detective put his hand out to pull it open in the opposite direction. Seth saw what was happening and backed out of the way to see who was going to win and go through the door first. Seth started to smile at Chloe until he saw her face.

"Chloe, what is wrong? You look as white as a ghost."

"You shook his hand. Why would you shake his hand? I can't believe you shook his hand!"

"Shook whose hand? What are you talking about? Who are you talking about?"

"I think you just shook hands with the man that has been stalking me."

All three of them backed out on to the street. Chloe quickly explained to them what had taken place. By the time she had fully explained what was going on it was too late for them to catch him. They tried. They listened to Chloe's description and then one ran in one direction and the other ran in the other direction, but neither one found anyone fitting the description she had given them. As they returned to the police station, they did find a jacket and a cap lying on the ground next to the sidewalk leading up to the station.

Once again, Detective Bonner thought this man was becoming too bold. Now it was as if he was taunting not only Mrs. Kelley, but the police department too. He picked up the jacket and the cap and decided to take them to forensics.

When Detective Bonner dropped off both items, all three of them went in search of Jo Ann. When they found her, she and Chloe went off by themselves to work on Chloe's sketch. As Jo Ann listened intently to what Chloe was saying, she tried to work her magic on the piece of paper in front of her.

They had been working for what seemed like hours, and Chloe didn't feel like they were making any progress at all. Jo Ann said she was doing fine, but Chloe could not seem to direct Jo Ann so she could get a likeness of the man she was pleased with. She had only seen him for a split second but felt like it was her fault they were not being successful.

Seth could tell Chloe was getting frustrated. She would stand up, then she would sit down, or she would pace back and forth wringing her hands the whole time. He knew her, and he knew her well. It was time for him to intervene. He went to the door and knocked quietly while at the same time opening the door and walking in.

"Chloe, I think it's time for you to take a break. Actually, why don't we call it quits for today? We'll come back tomorrow and you can try again. How does that sound?"

"What do you think, Detective Bonner?" Chloe said as she looked at the detective. "I really want to catch this guy, and I hate giving up, but I really am tired."

"I think that is probably a very good idea. Maybe you will think of something during the night that you didn't think of today. You never know what can happen so don't give up. I'll walk you to the door since I may as well go home too. It's been a long day."

They were all quiet as they walked toward the doors. Each one was deep in their own thoughts. The door opened and they parted ways. Detective Bonner forgot something in his desk so he turned around and went back into the station. It was two hours later before he actually left the station to head for home.

When he finally reached his car and put out his hand to open the door, that's when he saw the note written on his window. There were two simple words. *"She's mine."*

He reached for his cell phone and called forensics to tell them what he had seen and where he was parked.

He cordoned off the area securing it for the forensics team that was now on their way. He continued looking around to see if there was anyone or anything that should not be there. So far he had not found anything.

He saw the forensics team when they arrived, so he returned to his car.

"Thanks, Dave. I appreciate you getting here so fast. You can see the window for yourself, but I doubt if you will get anything from it. This man seems to be pretty good at covering his tracks or putting the blame on someone else, but I guess we can always hope."

"You go ahead and do what you need to do here and I'm going to continue to look around. I promise I won't get in your hair."

"I can't believe I shook that man's hand and now he has even left me a note on my car. He's getting bolder and evidently he wants Mrs. Kelley," Detective Bonner said to himself under his breath, as he continued to work the crime scene.

He had almost shaken Dave's hand when he had first arrived, but just in time he saw that Dave had already put his gloves on so he pulled back and just slapped him on the back. Detective Bonner then turned away and went back to policing the area around his car, but now he wasn't alone. Other police officers were now arriving. After talking to the detective, some stayed and helped him; others left returning to their desks. He knew too many people, police or not, could contaminate a crime scene and he needed a break of some kind on this case.

Detective Bonner very slowly went over the area in and around his car and did not find anything. Nothing at all except the note, and the note was written on the window.

What to do now? He hated to, but he guessed it was time to call Mr. and Mrs. Kelley. He had put it off as long as he could. Except for the note, there was nothing else he could tell them.

He picked up his cell phone and went to Mr. Kelley's number and pushed send. It rang and rang. Just as he was about to hang up Mrs. Kelley answered.

"Hello, Detective Bonner. We were out on the patio and didn't hear the phone ring. Seth usually keeps it with him, but I guess this time he forgot. How can we help you?"

"I guess you might as well put me on speaker phone that way I won't have to repeat everything I say to your husband, too."

After listening to the detective, Seth asked him a question. "How easy is it to get to your car, Detective?"

"It's not hard at all. The only thing that would be hard would be deciding whose car is whose. We're not a big station so there has never been a need for a lot of security."

After they finished listening, Seth and Chloe were in shock and did not know what to say or do. They thought it was over with the death of John Bledsoe but now it looked as if it was just beginning.

Chapter Twenty-Three

O nce again, the man was watching from the woods. Mr. and Mrs. Kelley were out on the patio when the phone rang. Mr. Kelley didn't hear it, but evidently Mrs. Kelley did because she jumped up and ran into the house leaving the patio door open. He heard Mrs. Kelley say Detective Bonner's name and when she said his name, Seth got up and went inside.

છ

He had gotten a thrill out of shaking Seth and Detective Bonner's hand. He had done it right in front of her while staring straight into her eyes. The look on her face when he waved was priceless. As soon as he turned the corner, he ran as fast as he could to put distance between them and him. While running he threw his cap and jacket on the ground. Throwing it by the sidewalk at the police station was a personal triumph. He knew he had gotten away and he grinned in anticipation of being able to return to the woods.

Things were definitely looking up. He continued to stand by the tree as he watched Seth and Chloe talking. When had he started calling them by their first names? He didn't really remember. It didn't matter though. He just didn't like getting too personal, but there was a certain feeling of power that you got when you knew the name of the intended victim.

He thought they might stay in the house after they finished talking to Detective Bonner, but they didn't. They came back out on the patio and sat down. They didn't say anything to each other; they just sat there. After several moments, Seth reached over and took Chloe's hand, they bowed their heads, and then he heard the word GOD. Then he heard Seth's voice loud and clear.

"Lord, this has been a fearful day and though we know in our hearts you have not given us a spirit of fear, but of a sound mind, it is hard to overcome the fear that has enveloped us. But once again we choose to put our lives in your hands. We ask your protection and guidance not only for what we say and do but also for Detective Bonner, because he needs a break so he can solve this case. In Jesus' name we pray. Amen."

CB

Once he heard the word GOD he crept closer so he could hear what was being said. He heard it all but he could not believe what he heard. "Did they actually believe there was a GOD and that He was going to help them?" He didn't care one bit about Seth, but he did want her.

He didn't believe in GOD, and all this praying made him nervous. He really didn't know why it made him nervous but it did. He now knew that Chloe was going to be his. For a while it seemed as if everything was getting in his way. But no more, because things seemed to be looking up and today had been a good day for him. He had enjoyed himself immensely. Whether they prayed or not she was going to be his.

CB

Seth and Chloe sat on the recliner together. The T.V. was on, but neither one of them could tell you what was actually playing; they were so engrossed in their own thoughts.

Seth was remembering the discussion he and Calvin had when they had first returned from overseas. It seemed like it had been forever, and it wasn't. Had it only been a couple of days? Surely not.

He really did understand Calvin's point of view. Calvin needed an employee who could actually work for the company. Chloe needed Seth more now than before. Seth was going to have to make a decision soon. He and Calvin were friends, but Calvin had a business to run and his problems were not Calvin's problems. He did have some vacation time saved up, but when that ran out, he would have to make a decision because he could not leave Calvin hanging not knowing what to do.

If he decided to quit, they would have no income and their savings would only last so long. If he found a job closer to home, that still wouldn't help because he would still have to leave her to go to work. There was one other option. They could sell this place and move to Houston. He would be able to keep his job and maybe the stalker would not be able to find them. They had lived in Houston before, but they really didn't want to live in a big city.

None of the options were very appealing so he would wait until his vacation time was up and make his decision then. He didn't think Chloe would like them either, but he didn't know what else to do.

Chloe was also thinking her own thoughts and they went right along with her husband's. If only they would catch this man, she could get back to her life. She got up and went to the kitchen to get herself a drink of water. She stood at the kitchen window and looked out into the woods. She had always loved the view, but right now she didn't like it so much. As she stood there, she wondered if he was out there watching her. For a moment she stood there not caring whether he was or not. She drank her water, put the glass in the dishwasher, and returned to the living room.

"Seth, would you come sit by the pool while I swim or better yet come swim with me."

"I'll come watch you, but right now I have some work I need to do on the computer for Calvin."

Chloe changed into her swimsuit, grabbed her towel, and headed for the swimming pool. She knew Seth wouldn't be long and she was eager to go for a swim. As she lowered herself in the pool, it felt so good. She started to swim and then she automatically went into her exercise mode. It had been a long time and it felt good to be in the water once again.

She had been swimming for a while, and Seth still wasn't in the chair where he usually sat. She called out, but he didn't answer. She just figured he couldn't hear her so she continued to swim deciding that if he didn't come in a little while, she would just go in.

After a few more laps, she decided to call it quits. Seth still hadn't come outside so she swam to the ladder and when she pulled herself up out of the water, she came face to face with the man who had been stalking her. He held a gun in his hand.

"Hello, Mrs. Kelley. Although I would much rather call you Chloe" Before he could finish talking Chloe screamed. He laughed and said, "No one is going to hear you. Your husband is lying on the patio floor and as you know, none of your neighbors are really that close. So get out of the pool. Now!"

Chloe did what she was told. As she did so, she felt him come up behind her as she went down the opposite side of the ladder. She tried to turn and fight, but he put something over her mouth and she felt herself losing consciousness. Her last thought was *"Oh, God. Help me!"*

Chapter Twenty-Four

Detective Bonner's cell phone rang. He looked at the display; it was Dave from forensics and he was hoping that he had something good to tell him.

"Dave, please tell me you have something for me."

"Today, Bob, I am going to make your day. Not that you'll actually be able to use it against your stalker in a court of law, but it does put him around your car. But with our parking area so open a lot of people have access to it also."

"Okay, spit it out. Who am I looking for?"

"His name is Sean Delaney."

"Where do I know that name from? I've heard it before, but I just can't place it."

"I can't help you there, Bob. All I know is his fingerprints showed up in AFIS, and his DNA matched up with the saliva that was found on the candy wrapper and cigarette butt."

"Thanks Dave. I appreciate your help and I more than appreciate you getting back to me so fast. Thanks a lot. At least now I have something to work with."

The first thing Detective Bonner did when he went back in the station was to ask everyone around him if they had ever heard of Sean Delaney. No one had.

Detective Bonner sat at his desk with his chair pushed back so he was balancing on the back two legs. He put his hands behind his neck interlacing his fingers and closed his eyes. Those who knew him knew better than to bother him because he was deep in thought.

After several minutes, he smiled and allowed the front legs of his chair to plop down on the floor making so much noise that everyone glanced in his direction. Seeing his smile everyone around him knew he had come up with the answer he was seeking. Some of them started his way to ask him, but he picked up his cell phone so they turned around and went back to their desks.

"Julie, how are you feeling today?" He said as his wife answered the phone.

"As well as can be expected, for an extremely pregnant lady. What's up?"

"I know this may seem to be a very strange question, but I really need to know the answer. I am hoping you will remember our conversation and be able to help me."

"I'll try." Julie said as she listened to her husband.

"I seem to remember a few months ago you and one of your friends went to a mall close to Houston. I don't remember who you went with or what mall you went to, but I remember you said you both got tired and went to the food court. You sat down and saved a table while your friend went to get the food."

"Okay," Julie said. "I'm not quite understanding where you are going with this."

"Listen, this is the important part. You said your friend had accidently left her wallet on the counter and one of the employees brought it to your table to give it back. When he handed the wallet to her, he then turned and hit on you for a date. Now this is really important. Do you remember his name?"

"I'm not sure," Julie said. "Hold on just a minute and let me think. Several minutes passed. "Bob, I think I do remember. It was

John something. No it wasn't. It was Sean something. Sean, John, Sean? It was Sean. Yes, that's it. Sean. Sean Delaney. He was creepy. I don't mean to be mean, but I haven't been back to the mall since because of him."

"Okay, one more question. Do you remember what your order was?"

"I don't remember the name of the place, but I'm pretty sure it was Mexican food. We always get Mexican food when I go shopping with anyone. I'm pretty sure it was the mall in Humble. Not positive, but pretty sure."

"Thanks, Julie. You've helped me more than you know. Be sure you take it easy and I'll talk to you later. Bye, Honey."

Detective Bonner got up from his desk and went out to his car. He decided to call Seth Kelley's cell phone but didn't get an answer. He waited several minutes and called again. He then decided to call his home phone and again he didn't answer. He was becoming concerned because he knew that with all that was going on in their lives Seth would not be where he could not answer one phone or the other.

He tried one more time and not getting an answer he headed toward the Kelley's house with lights flashing. As Detective Bonner pulled up in front of the Kelley's house, he noticed the garage door was open and Mrs. Kelley's car was gone, but Seth's car was still there. It seemed strange they would leave the garage door open because they hadn't done that in a long time.

He got out of his car and went to the front door. He rang the doorbell several times but no one came to the door so he decided to look around. He went back to the garage and went inside. It smelled a little funny but other than that nothing was amiss. Then he went around to the side of the house and saw Seth lying on the floor in front of the patio door and the patio door was wide open.

He pulled his cell phone out and called 911. Seth was unconscious and lying in a large pool of blood. It looked like he had been there for some time. Hating to disturb the crime scene, but knowing if he didn't get Seth in the house, his chance of survival was in jeopardy. So checking him over to make sure it wouldn't hurt him Detective Bonner pulled Seth as far as he could into the house.

Once inside the detective did all he could to stop the flow of blood from a wound on Seth's head. He had also been stabbed, and he couldn't tell which wound was worse. Both wounds were bleeding profusely so he got two towels from the kitchen and put pressure on each wound the best he could. Finally he heard the ambulance siren in the distance. He knew it would take them several more minutes so he began to pray. Seth didn't look good at all and there was so much blood.

As the ambulance pulled up to the side of the house, Detective Bonner yelled out the back door telling them where to go. The first paramedic ran to him; while the second one backed the ambulance closer to the patio and then he jumped out and ran to help.

Both paramedics worked together as they stabilized Seth enough so he could be transported to the hospital. He was still unconscious so they put him on a stretcher, put him in the ambulance, closed the doors, and headed toward the hospital with Detective Bonner right behind.

While the paramedics worked on Seth, Detective Bonner looked everywhere for Mrs. Kelley. He found a rag on the ground between the swimming pool and the patio and figured that Sean Delaney used it to incapacitate Mrs. Kelley and then kidnapped her. Probably in her own car since it was missing.

He called the station and put out an APB on her car and for now that was all he could do. He needed more than anything to talk to Mr. Kelley, but for the time being that was impossible.

Chapter Twenty-Five

C hloe woke up and she was lying on a bed. Her hands and feet were tied and she had some duct tape over her mouth. She tried to move but she couldn't and she couldn't figure out why. It was so dark in the room she couldn't see anything so she just laid there trying to get her eyes to adjust.

ଓ

He watched her from the next room. He had put a large two-way mirror between the two rooms several weeks ago just for this day. He sat and watched her all night long even though she was unconscious. He didn't care; she was his now and no one was going to take her away. As he watched, he thought he could detect some movement. Last night when he saw her move, he had gone in and put more chloroform on the rag which put her back to sleep. Now he decided it was time for her to wake up. He opened the door where she was, slipped his hand in and turned on the light, hoping it would encourage her to wake up.

ଓ

Chloe tried to get her wits about her as she lay there. She kept her eyes closed so if whoever had taken her was watching, he would think she was still asleep. She was alone and she was afraid. She tried to tell herself she wasn't; but she was. In her darkest moment, once again she called out to God. She knew it may not feel like He was there, but she knew He was and she knew He would never leave nor forsake her. But what if He decided it was time for her to go be with Him? She didn't really want to die, but she knew if it was her time, it was her time. It was hard to come to that point but she did. She was a child of the living God and she chose to put her life in His hands. She had done it many times before, but never before had she felt it so deep in her soul. She was at peace and no matter the consequences; she belonged to Him.

☙

The doctor had taken Seth to surgery as soon as the ambulance arrived. They tried very hard to save him and after several hours in the operating room, they finally succeeded. He was in ICU and unconscious, but he was alive.

Detective Bonner put a policeman in front of Seth's door just to be on the safe side, but he didn't really think he was in danger because Sean Delaney had what he wanted.

Detective Bonner stayed at the hospital until Mr. Kelley was out of the operating room. He really wanted to talk to him but was informed they were going to keep him sedated for a while. As he sat there waiting for Seth to regain consciousness, he decided it might be a good idea for him to go talk to Mrs. Bellamy and see if she and Mrs. Kelley had been shopping in Humble at any time.

After he left the hospital, Detective Bonner pulled up behind Mrs. Bellamy's car just as she was getting ready to leave. "Hello, Detective Bonner, what can I do for you?"

"I don't know if you know it or not, but Mr. Kelley is in the hospital and we believe Mrs. Kelley has been kidnapped. I would like to ask you some questions to see if maybe I can get a lead so we can find her."

"Of course, Detective, would you like to come in while we talk?"

"I was going to say no, but this might turn into more than I think depending on your answers to my questions."

Darla and Detective Bonner turned around and went into the house. Darla indicated he should sit in one of the living room chairs and then asked him if he would like something to drink.

"I don't think so, Mrs. Bellamy. I think it would be better if we get right to the point. Mrs. Kelley's life may depend on it.

"Ask away, Detective. I would like to help in anyway that I can."

"You know what has been going on at the Kelley's. You've even been part of some of it. I would like to know if you know a man by the name of Sean Delaney?"

Darla sat there. She knew the name sounded familiar but she didn't know why. "Let me think for a minute. I know I've heard it, but I just can't remember where."

They sat there for several minutes as Darla tried to remember where she had heard the name.

"I'm sorry, Detective. I just can't remember. It's so frustrating because I know I've heard it. I just can't place where. I am so sorry. I know how important it is."

Detective Bonner got up to leave thanking Mrs. Bellamy for her time and then started toward the door. He had already got to his car and was opening his car door when Darla came running out.

"Detective, I remember. Thank you, Lord. I remember. Please come back in and I'll tell you all I know."

Darla and the Detective went back in the house and she proceeded to tell him what she knew.

"Chloe and I went to the mall in Humble. Actually, I think Connie went with us too, but I'm not for sure. We shopped until lunchtime then went to the food court to get something to eat."

"We found a table, put our packages under it, and I believe Chloe and Connie went and found us some Mexican food. We always eat Mexican food. No, Connie wasn't there, and I went and got the food because Chloe was too tired. Then a man came up just before we finished eating and said his name was Sean Delaney and he worked for the Mexican place where I had just bought our food. He had my wallet in his hand. He said I had left it on the counter and since my driver's license was on the outside, he looked around the food court and spotted us. So he brought it over, and I thanked him. I told him how much I appreciated him returning it and offered him a tip. He refused then turned around and left. For some reason I seem to remember he hit on Chloe, but that part I'm not really sure about."

"That's it. Do you think he's the one that kidnapped her?"

At that moment, Detective Bonner's cell phone rang. He listened for a moment then said, "Thank you, Doctor. I am glad to hear that. I'll be there as fast as I can."

The detective looked at Mrs. Bellamy saying, "Seth has regained consciousness. He's still a little groggy but I'm hoping by the time I get there he will be able to talk to me. Thank you for your help, Mrs. Bellamy."

He got up, shook Darla's hand, and headed for her front door. Darla grabbed her purse and also headed for the front door, "Detective Bonner I was headed out to run some errands when you pulled up behind me, but after I am finished do you think it is too early to visit Seth?"

"I'm pretty sure it's too early. I would give him at least a day or two, and even then you should probably call ahead to make sure before you make the trip." On finishing his sentence, the detective got in his car and headed to the hospital. Darla got in her car and left to do her errands.

When he got to the highway, Detective Bonner called his partner, Tim Roberts, and gave him the information he had gleaned from Mrs. Bellamy. Once he had told him all he knew about the case, he disconnected the call, and continued on to the hospital while his mind was still going a mile a minute.

Once Detective Roberts received the information from Detective Bonner, he started following up immediately. He found the name of the Mexican food place and put in a call. The manager wasn't there at the moment, but an employee had taken Detective Roberts number and promised to have him call as soon as he returned.

Upon returning to the hospital Detective Bonner walked into Seth's room. He was awake and in a lot of pain, but more importantly he was afraid for his wife.

"Please, Detective, tell me that you have found her."

"I wish I could, Seth. We do have a pretty good lead, but that's all. Actually, we have two."

"Seth, can you tell me what happened?"

"I wish I knew. All I remember is getting hit on the head. I think I also remember getting stabbed, but I don't really remember whether it was before or after I got hit. Chloe told me she was going for a swim. I was going to get my laptop and follow her out. I couldn't find it so it took me a little longer than I expected and because it had taken me longer I was really uncomfortable about leaving her alone for so long. I ran out the patio door and ran right into this guy's knife. I didn't fall immediately so he hit me on the head."

"I don't know what happened, but I did come to for a minute and I saw Chloe on his shoulder as he was heading for the edge of the house where the garage is. I yelled at him and tried to get up and that's when he shot me. After that, I don't remember anything until I woke up here in the hospital."

"Not much help, huh?"

"You said you were shot. I didn't know you were shot. Why didn't someone tell me you were shot?"

"I don't know, Detective, I just know I was. Maybe because it was just a flesh wound and the other two were more important."

"Maybe so, but I should have been told. I just wanted to let you know what is going on. Just keep on praying."

"I am, Detective. Ever since I woke up, I have been praying non stop. Go, do what you need to do. I want my wife back."

Detective Bonner walked out of Seth's room, then out of the hospital and toward his car. On returning to the station, he went in search of his partner.

When Detective Roberts saw his partner approaching, he put his hands up in the air with a small shrug and told him the restaurant owner had not called him back.

"What's the number of the restaurant and the manager's name?"

"Mr. Donovan, this is Detective Bonner of the Police Department. I believe my partner, Detective Roberts, has tried three times to contact you by phone and all three times you were unavailable; but we were assured that you would return the call. You did not."

"Mr. Donovan, this is a kidnapping and assault investigation. You can either answer my questions over the phone or I'm sure the Humble police department will be happy to come and get you and ask you the questions themselves."

Detective Bonner wasn't sure they would be happy to help or not, but hopefully Mr. Donovan didn't know that either. He waited as Mr. Donovan made his decision and thankfully, he decided to answer the questions over the phone.

"Can you tell me if you have or if you ever have had a man by the name of Sean Delaney working for you?"

"I can tell you he doesn't work for us now, but I know he did a few months or even weeks ago. If you will give me your number, I will check our records and call you back."

"No, Mr. Donovan, I think I will wait right here while you go look."

Mr. Donovan had worked for the company for two years, but it had only been part time. But now, he was a full time employee and had been made manager. So being the manager, he went and found Sean Delaney's file and returned to the phone asking Detective Bonner what he needed to know.

"Do you have an address for Sean Delaney? And if you do, what is it?"

"Yes, Detective, I do."

After finding out what the address was, both Detectives ran to their car and peeled out of the parking lot.

Chapter Twenty-Six

C hloe was up and walking around. She was very upset. As he watched her pace, he came to the conclusion he should not have untied her. Yes, he had the gun, but he didn't want to hurt her.....yet.

"What was she doing? Oh, no, not again." The man said as he watched her through the mirror.

Chloe had gone down on her knees. He knew she was praying. Did she not realize he had her, she could not get away, and he was in charge. God was not going to help her. She was really making him mad.

"She's mine, she's mine, she's mine. Not yours, Mr. Kelley. Not yours, God. But mine, all mine?" he screamed as he watched her pray.

Chloe heard the key in the lock. She jumped up and faced the door. *"Yea, though I walk through the valley of the shadow of death-------."* She stopped. He was in the room. Sean Delaney pointed the gun at her as he entered the room.

"Hello, Mrs. Kelley."

"Who are you? I don't know you."

"Yes, Mrs. Kelley, you do. Think back several months ago."

"I am sure I have never seen you before in my life."

Sean was getting angry. After all he had been through setting all this up, and she didn't even remember him.

"I'll give you a hint, Mrs. Kelley. The mall in Humble."

Chloe shook her head. "Nope."

"Mrs. Kelley, I returned your friend's wallet."

"And why did you have my friend's wallet?"

Sean was getting madder by the minute.

"Mrs. Kelley, she lost her wallet at the food court. I found it and brought it back to her."

"Yes, I think I vaguely remember that happening. I just don't remember you."

"Vaguely? What do you mean vaguely? From that day forward I decided you were going to be mine. Not his, mine."

"Sean, did you not notice I am married?" Chloe said as she held up her left hand to show him her wedding ring. That was when she noticed it was no longer there.

"What have you done with my wedding ring?"

"You don't need it anymore because you now belong to me."

"Just because I don't have my ring on doesn't mean I am going to belong to you. I will never belong to you."

"When your husband dies, if he's not already dead, then you will be free to be mine."

"What do you mean, when my husband dies? If he's not already dead? What have you done to him?"

Sean laughed as he continued to keep the gun pointed at her.

"I guess you weren't conscious at that point were you? Well, you see I stabbed him when he came running out your patio door. Then I hit him over the head, and then when he tried to come help you I shot him."

Tears welled up in Chloe's eyes as she sat down on the edge of the bed. She couldn't believe Seth was dead. She looked at Sean Delaney and she was filled with so much anger that she jumped up and lowered her head as if she was a bull in a bullfight and head butted him in the stomach.

He had already pointed his gun at her, but it went flying as her head came in contact with his stomach. It went off and both she and Sean fell to the floor.

ଔ

Detective Bonner and Detective Roberts were on the way to Sean Delaney's address. They didn't know if they were going to be on time or not, but they still had to try. Just as they pulled up in front of the Delaney home, they heard a gunshot. Both Detectives ran from their car to the house and busted in the front door.

They cleared each room before they went on to the next. There were only two rooms left. Detective Roberts took one and Detective Bonner took the other. On the count of three they each entered the room that was in front of them.

Detective Robert's room was empty, but it was the one that had the very large two-way mirror in it and he could see into the other room. He saw Detective Bonner just as he crashed through the door. Detective Bonner's room had both Sean Delaney and Chloe lying on the floor covered in blood.

Detective Bonner went to Delaney first, since he was lying on top of Chloe and felt for a pulse. He didn't find one. So feeling as if he had failed Chloe, he bent to check her pulse, and just as he touched her neck her eyes popped open.

"What took you so long?" she said as she tried to push Delaney off of her so she could breathe.

Seeing that Chloe was alive was a great relief to Detective Bonner, and he yelled at Detective Roberts to come help him get Delaney off of her. Delaney was a big man and it took both of them to set her free of his weight.

The ambulance arrived just as the detectives reached down to help her up.

"I'm pretty sure none of this blood is mine," she said as the paramedics entered the room.

"It may not be, but I think it would be a good idea for you to get checked out anyway. Just to make sure." Detective Bonner said as he backed out of the way allowing them to do their job.

"Before we go any further or say anything else I want to know if my husband is alive?"

"Yes, Mrs. Kelley, your husband is alive. It was touch and go for awhile, but he is going to make it." Detective Bonner said as he looked at Detective Roberts. "Tim, if you'll finish up here? I'll take Mrs. Kelley to the hospital and I will meet you at the station later?" The paramedics finished checking out Mrs. Kelley and turned toward the ambulance when Detective Bonner stopped them asking them if it was alright if Chloe could change her clothes in the ambulance before they left. Since they agreed, Detective Bonner went to his car and got out a spare pair of sweats he kept there and handed them to her.

Once she changed her clothes, she put them in the paper sacks Detective Bonner handed to her. Then she and the detective headed toward his car. He put the paper bags in the trunk and closed it. Then he walked her to the passenger side of the car and opened the door so she could get in and as he did, he said, "You have had a very long day, Mrs. Kelley. Why don't we get you to the hospital?"

"Detective Bonner, I cannot think of anything I would like more right now."

Shutting the door behind her, Detective Bonner stood there for a moment. His eyes went to the house as he took a last look at what was taking place. Yes, it had been a very long day.

He started toward his side of the car and all of a sudden, he had the oddest sensation. He opened the door on his side of the car and took a long look into the shadows of the trees that surrounded the house. The hairs on the back of his neck were standing straight up.

As he stood there for several seconds, he finally shook his head, rubbed the back of his neck, and got in the car deciding he was just tired.

Neither Chloe nor Detective Bonner was in a talkative mood so on the way to the hospital all was quiet in the car, which allowed each one to think their own thoughts. The quiet finally overtook Chloe and she fell into a light sleep.

After pulling up in front of the hospital and helping Mrs. Kelley out, Detective Bonner had one last thought as the hospital doors opened in front of them.

"Why had Sean Delaney been so fixated on Mrs. Kelley?" How had John Bledsoe fit into the scheme of things? And the feeling on the back of his neck just before they headed to the hospital. Where did that come from?" He had more questions than he had answers.

The policeman was still stationed in front of Seth's door. Chloe opened it slowly and peeked in just in case he was asleep. Seth was sitting on the edge of the bed looking straight at the door. As he caught sight of her, all the sadness disappeared from his eyes.

She walked to him and let him slowly and carefully pull her into his arms.

"I love you, Chloe"

"I love you too, Seth."

Epilogue

Chloe showed up at the hospital early on the morning Seth was being released. He was getting to come home today and she wanted to be there so she could help him get ready.

She pulled into the parking lot, found a spot to park, got her husband's clothes from the back seat, and then headed toward the door.

She had thanked God every morning for her life and the life of her husband. She knew He had been with her, but she had not been positive of its outcome.

She trusted God with all her heart, but even in having that trust, it did not always mean the outcome was the one you wanted. It meant God was with you no matter the outcome.

Chloe stood in front of Seth's door thankful it was no longer guarded by the policeman. He was asleep and his face was turned toward the door. She stood there staring at his face until he opened his eyes and looked straight at her. He smiled, "What are you standing out there for? Get yourself in here so I can finally get out of here."

She stepped toward the bed and took Seth's face in between her two hands and with a smile, she put her lips on his. With a quiet sigh she said, "I love you."

"Me, too."

The hospital insisted that Seth leave the hospital in a wheel chair. So once he was dressed and sitting in it, Chloe ran downstairs to the car so she could pull up to the front door. One of the nurses was going to bring him down and then they would head for home. Home, she loved the sound of that word.

www.ingramcontent.com/pod-product-compliance
Lightning Source LLC
Chambersburg PA
CBHW051258170626
46809CB00004B/1711